Dear Reader,

I hope you enjoy *Her Prince's Secret Son*. The idea
for this book first came to me as a regular secret-
baby story—you know, the kind where the heroine
has kept the child secret from the hero. But the
more I thought about the story, the more I realized
I wanted to do something different. So I decided
the hero would be the one who had kept the baby
a secret. But how in the world was such a thing
possible? After all, the man wouldn't be pregnant or
giving birth. It took a while to give my characters
the right backgrounds and situations to make a
reverse secret-baby story line work, but finally
the warrior prince and his commoner bookshop
owner appeared. From there, I had a great time
creating a popular fantasy—a regular girl discovers
her true love is a real prince, only this prince has
possession of the son she gave up for adoption.

I love hearing from readers. If you like
*Her Prince's Secret Son*, please write and let
me know. I can be reached through my Web site,
www.lindagoodnight.com.

Warm wishes

*Linda Goodnight*

# LINDA GOODNIGHT

*Her Prince's Secret Son*

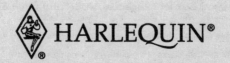

TORONTO • NEW YORK • LONDON
AMSTERDAM • PARIS • SYDNEY • HAMBURG
STOCKHOLM • ATHENS • TOKYO • MILAN • MADRID
PRAGUE • WARSAW • BUDAPEST • AUCKLAND

Recycling programs
for this product may
not exist in your area.

ISBN-13: 978-0-373-17639-7

HER PRINCE'S SECRET SON

First North American Publication 2010.

Copyright © 2009 by Linda Goodnight.

www.eHarlequin.com

**Printed in U.S.A.**

Winner of a RITA® Award for excellence in inspirational fiction, **Linda Goodnight** has also won a Booksellers' Best Award, ACFW Book of the Year, and a Reviewers' Choice Award from *RT Book Reviews*. Linda has appeared on the Christian bestseller list and her romance novels have been translated into more than a dozen languages. Active in orphan ministry, this former nurse and teacher enjoys writing fiction that carries a message of hope and light in a sometimes dark world. She and husband Gene live in Oklahoma. Readers can write to her at linda@lindagoodnight.com.

# A special bonus from Linda…
## Linda's Ten Rules for Dating a Prince

1. When talking to the press, smile, look stunning and don't tell them anything.

2. Never eat spinach or drink grape juice before a photo session.

3. Practice your curtsy so you don't tumble to the floor like a drunk monkey when meeting his parents for the first time.

4. And speaking of getting drunk, don't.

5. Wear a dress heavier than your crown so you aren't top-heavy.

6. Let the prince think he's always right. *You* know, of course, that he isn't. Don't ruin his fantasy.

7. Do not ask the prince's mother if she would like to see your skull-and-crossbones tattoo. Trust me—she wouldn't.

8. Memorize the names of the first 150 people in line for the throne. Do not allow any of these people to serve refreshments to the prince (unless he's been really, really naughty).

9. Learn to dance backward in high heels while smiling and carrying on a conversation with sweaty old men who reek of mothballs. They probably hold the country's purse strings.

10. Last, but of utmost importance, be ready and willing to produce heirs to the throne, preferably male, and then return to a size-four dress the day after delivery.

# CHAPTER ONE

PRINCE ALEKSANDRE D' GABRIEL took one look at Dr. Konstantine's long face and knew the news was bad.

"I'm sorry, Your Majesty, there is nothing more I can do." The royal physician, either unable or unwilling to meet his prince's eyes, stared down at the gleaming marble floor. "Your son is dying."

The softly spoken words pierced Aleks's soul like a bayonet. His boy, his reason for living, lay just beyond the thick, ancient castle wall dying, while his father stood in the long, ornate corridor of Carvainian Castle wishing to die in his stead.

Aleks was a ruler, a warrior prince, a man of wealth and power, and yet he was helpless against the infection that was destroying his son's internal organs.

He clenched his fists against the rising tide of fear, stifling the urge to pummel the stone walls in frustration and despair.

His mother, Queen Irena, touched his arm. "There must be something more we can do. Perhaps another physician?"

Dr. Konstantine's head jerked upward. "Your Highness, we've consulted every hepatology specialist in the world. The only answer is an organ donation. A tiny piece of organ from the right person will save his life. Nothing more, nothing less."

Queen Irena's face, still lovely though she was nearing sixty, had aged in the past weeks of Prince Nico's illness. The lines around her mouth deepened as she said, "My apologies, Doctor, I didn't mean to imply anything less than the best on your part. It's just that—" She lifted one hand in a helpless gesture.

Aleksandre understood exactly what she was feeling. The queen doted on the motherless boy she'd carried in her arms from America nearly five years ago. Without his mother's help, Aleksandre would never have known his son.

Fate and determination had given him Nico, and he would not give up his child without a fight.

"There must be a match somewhere," he said. "We will continue our search."

"Thousands have been tested, Your Majesty."

His people, loyal Carvainians, had lined the streets and clogged the telephones and computers in their sincere desire to save the adored little prince. But not a single person was a suitable match for the child whose blood was not one hundred percent Carvainian.

Aleksandre fought the sickness churning in his gut and the memory of an American woman who still haunted his heart. The child's mixed blood was his fault, just as the illness was, and yet Nico would not be Nico without Sara Presley's blood.

"I have a suggestion." Dr. Konstantine's gaze skittered away only to return with a fresh boldness. "May I speak frankly?"

The prince gave a bark of mirthless laughter. Dr. Konstantine had tended him for years, through childhood illnesses and wartime wounds. He trusted the man implicitly. "I have yet to quell your propensity for doing so. And we now are at a point of desperate measures. Say your piece."

"Nico's birth mother."

"No!" At the queen's outcry, both Prince Aleksandre and

the physician turned to stare. Her face had gone white, and the long, graceful fingers pressed against her lips trembled. Aleks understood her reluctance for it matched his own, and yet, had he not just been thinking of Sara Presley?

"She won't agree." A deep and dreadful knot formed in his chest at the thought of the woman who had jilted him and abandoned their child. She had no love for either the father or the son. She had not cared then. She would not care now if Nico lived or died.

The physician pressed. "You have no other choice but to contact her, Your Majesty. She is the little prince's last hope."

The queen regained her voice. Her nails scraped against Aleksandre's sleeve. Almost feverishly she said, "Listen to me, Aleksandre. The woman has a heart of stone. She will never agree. Contacting her can only bring trouble that we do not need. Our burdens are heavy enough to bear. Think of the consequences. Think of what she might require of you. Of your son."

Aleksandre knew his mother was right. Sara Presley had damaged him before, but now, with Nico as a pawn, she might try to exact a price he was unwilling to pay. And yet, what choice did they have?

Dr. Konstantine was like a dog with a bone—or a man with no other recourse. "If she is a match, she could be the answer to our prayers."

"*If* she is a match, and *if* she would agree," Aleksandre said grimly. So many ifs. A woman who would abandon her newborn was not likely to go through surgery on his behalf…unless she had a strong incentive.

Queen Irena paced to the sunlit patch at the end of the hallway. She spun toward him, her agitation showing in jerky movements and the rapid rise and fall of silk over her breasts. "I won't have her here, Aleksandre. She's poison. She'll hurt us. Hurt you. Hurt Nico. I can't bear to watch that happen again."

The prince held up a hand. "Stop. This is my decision. Let me think."

Both his companions bowed slightly and grew silent. His mother's soulful black eyes watched him, reproachful. A twinge of guilt niggled at his conscience.

If not for the Queen Mother, Carvainia would have no Crown Prince Nico, and he would have no son. No one, other than himself, understood the treachery of Sara Presley as well as Mother. She was trying to protect both of her princes as she always had.

Aleksandre closed his eyes tightly for a brief moment to calm his raging spirit. He'd learned in battle to shut out the noise and horror around him and go deep inside to a place of peace where wisdom lived. He did that now, weeding out his own anguish at the thought of seeing Sara Presley again and concentrated instead on saving his child.

Vaguely, he could hear the quiet hush of servants moving about the castle and of nurses moving in and out of Nico's room. He listened deeper, imagined the sounds of the sea just outside the castle walls.

The sea was his solace and when time allowed he walked the beach to taste the salt spray on his tongue and smell the wind blowing across the great water. Someday he would teach Nico to sail and fish and race his speedboats. He would tell his son stories of the generations of Carvainians who had used the sea for defense and trade and livelihood.

But first, his son must live. And to live, he must have an organ donation. And that could only come from his biological mother.

He took a deep, cleansing breath and opened his eyes, certain now of what he must do.

"You are correct, Mother, when you say that the American woman will not come willingly. I also agree with you, Doctor, that she is our only hope. She must come." His jaw hardened with resolve. "She *will* come."

Queen Irena tossed her head. "You cannot force her. She is not under Carvainian jurisdiction."

"Not yet." A sly smile touched his bitter-tasting lips. "But she will be."

The queen's eyes widened. "Aleksandre, whatever are you thinking?"

"The American woman will not come to Carvainia for me or even for her son, but she will come if the incentive is great enough."

"And you will see that it is?"

"I know exactly what matters most to Sara Presley."

As a prince who'd led men into battle, he knew the importance of strategy and of knowing one's enemy.

And so a battle plan was forged.

"If something sounds too good to be true, it probably is," Sara Presley said with a laugh as she unpacked a box of novels for the romance section of The Book Shelf.

"But what if the prize is real, Sara?" Penny Carter, her friend and business partner waved the letter beneath Sara's nose for the umpteenth time in two days. "What if you've really won a fabulous trip to a European health spa—in a castle, no less?"

Sara scoffed. "To win, I would have to enter, right?"

"Well, maybe, but we own a bookstore. What if one of our vendors is rewarding us for outstanding sales?"

"Then you would be included in the trip. And you're not." Sara held a new book to her nose and sniffed.

"I love that smell," she said, trying to direct Penny's thoughts somewhere besides the goofy award letter. It couldn't be real. The prize was either a joke, or when she called, they'd ask her to send thousands of dollars or to provide her credit card number. She wasn't that stupid.

But as she'd done all morning, Penny stayed after her. "What about those contests you signed up for at the fair last month?"

Sara paused in thought, gazing down at a book cover. A shirtless cowboy gave her a sexy grin but she didn't feel a thing. No matter how sexy or how nice, no man had gotten past her defenses in over five years. She was a strong advocate of "once burned, twice warned."

"Cassie Binger won a blender at the fair last year," she mused, "so I guess that's possible."

Penny let out a whoop, pounding her index finger at the letter. "Call this number, right now, before I die of curiosity." She patted a hand over her heart. The letter crinkled against her plaid shirt. "Castle-by-the-Sea Health and Beauty Spa sounds so romantic."

"The only place I'll find romance is between the covers of the books we sell. The letter is a scam, Penny. It has to be. My luck ran out a long time ago." She quickly turned to the wall-high bookshelves.

Penny marched around to her side. Hands on her hips she said, "Sara, listen to me. You've spent five years living in the past. Five years haunting the Internet in hopes of finding out who adopted your baby. Five years getting over the jerk who left you."

Tears welled in Sara's eyes. Her belly gnawed with emptiness now as it did every time she thought of the infant son she'd lost. And she thought of him constantly. A TV show, a book cover, a child on the street or in the store could send her into a tailspin for days. "Don't, Penny."

Penny grasped Sara's upper arms and pulled her around, her face wreathed in compassion. "Honey, I'm not trying to hurt you. You're my best friend and I love you like a sister. But I've watched you beat yourself up for too long. When life offers sunshine, don't hide in the shade. You have to move on."

"I can't, Penny." She sniffed. "My baby is out there somewhere. Is he happy and healthy? Does his adoptive mother love him the way I do?"

"You made the right choice. You did what was best for him at the time. Let it go. Move on. Let yourself live again."

They'd hashed this through hundreds of times and Sara knew Penny was right. Penniless, without family to turn to, and still in college on scholarship, she'd done what she had to in order to secure her baby's future. "I'm haunted by the thought that if I'd kept him, something would have worked out."

"If that Aleks jerk had stuck around and been the man you thought he was, things would have worked out. But he didn't. That's my point. Life happened. It sucks but it happened. Now, life is happening again in a good way." She shoved the letter at Sara. "Take a chance, Sara. Go for it. Just this once, let yourself be happy."

Sara shook her head but took the letter in hand. Penny's insistence was starting to wear her down. She did need a change. She needed to shake loose from the guilt and loss and depression that had plagued her for too long.

In a feeble attempt to resist, she muttered, "It can't be true. I wish it was, but I'm not the kind of person who wins fabulous trips to Europe."

A male voice intruded. "I beg to differ, Miss Presley. If you are indeed Sara Presley, you are our grand prize winner."

Both women spun toward the tall, imposing figure who had entered the shop. Dressed in a business suit with hair graying at the temples and the smell of intellect coming off him in waves, the man reminded her of a slick television lawyer.

"Who are you?" Sara blurted. "And how do you know about the prize?"

"I am here as executor of the contest, Miss Presley. Since you have not yet called to claim your prize, the owner of the spa felt an official visit was in order to assure you that everything is in order and that our staff eagerly awaits your arrival."

Sara looked from the man to Penny. Her friend's eyes were as round as saucers.

"Are you serious?" Sara gestured to the letter. "This is for real?"

"Indeed." The man moved into the small space behind the cluttered counter and offered Sara a manila envelope. "Inside you will find a brochure detailing the prize, a round-trip ticket and your cash prize."

"Cash?" Sara squeaked. "Ticket?"

With hands now trembling, she removed the items from the envelope one by one. Penny leaned over her shoulder. "That stuff's real, Sara."

"I can't believe this." She read over the brochure and saw photos of pampered women getting massages and facials, of a fabulous castle standing proud and ancient by a perfect blue sea, of rooms so beautiful they stole her breath. She checked the airline ticket. Her stomach jumped into her throat. "First class?"

"A vacation unrivaled by any other awaits you, miss, a once-in-a-lifetime opportunity." The man tilted his head. "Do you believe it now?"

"I'm beginning to."

"Excellent. I will tell the owner of Castle-by-the-Sea to expect you. He will be delighted to greet you on Thursday."

Sara trailed him as he moved toward the door. "Thursday? This coming Thursday? That's only two days away."

"Why, yes, madam. Is that a problem?"

Penny popped up behind them and gave Sara a little whack on the shoulder. "No problem at all. She'll be there."

Two days later Sara was still in delighted shock as she waved goodbye to a jubilant Penny and boarded a plane for London. Once there, she was whisked aboard a private jet that took her to Castle-by-the-Sea.

As she disembarked, she breathed in the scent of sea spray, warm and salty and so different from the landlocked aroma of Kansas.

At the bottom of the steps, a line of attendants waited, tidy and professional in red uniforms. The castle itself sprawled before her, a stunning old stone structure complete with spires and cupolas and towers that had no doubt once housed European royalty. In the distance, below the hill was a blue sea that would have provided protection for the castle inhabitants. Today a handful of people reclined on the white sand or cavorted in the crystal waters.

The butterflies in her belly fluttered. "This must be a resort for the rich and famous."

She pinched herself. Surely there was a mistake. She was a nobody. Surely she would be sent packing by nightfall.

But that was not the case. She was escorted to a private suite high in one wing of the castle, and for the rest of the afternoon she was fed and massaged, pampered and waited upon so that when night came she fell asleep in the canopied bed with a smile on her face. Maybe her run of bad luck was finally over.

* * *

"Miss Presley. Miss Presley." A woman's accented voice penetrated the fog in Sara's brain.

"I'm Sara. Just Sara," she muttered, though her throat was froggy with sleep. She snuggled deeper into the smooth, silken sheets and pulled the down comforter up to her ears. She'd been having the loveliest dream ever.

"Well, 'Just Sara.' The intruding voice sounded amused. "I take it you slept well."

Sara sat up straight and stared around the luxurious room and then at the young woman whom she recognized as Antonia, her personal attendant. "I wasn't dreaming. This is real."

"Yes, miss. Very real. Would you care for breakfast before we begin the day?"

"Coffee please."

From a pretty tray, the round-figured Antonia poured the fragrant coffee and handed it to Sara. "Not a very healthy beginning to a busy day. Some melon perhaps? Or strawberries and cream? That seems to be a favorite with our guests. We grow our own, you see."

"The strawberries or the cream?"

"Both." The young woman giggled.

Feeling a little like Cinderella, Sara laughed with her. "What's on the agenda for today?"

Something shifted through Antonia's soft brown eyes. Sara noticed the slight hesitation and wondered. But before her thoughts could wander too far, the attendant smiled and the expression disappeared. "A very special treat awaits you. The owner of Castle-by-the-Sea wishes to see you."

"I was hoping you'd say that. I really want to thank him."

Antonia gazed at her a second longer before turning away.

Within the hour Sara was dressed and standing outside an enormous pair of ornate double doors inside a palace of such breathtaking beauty, it must be a tourist attraction. From the looks of this particular wing—one of many from what she'd observed so far—and the scurry of suit-clad men and women going in and out of offices, this was the business section of the spa. Apparently behind these white and gilded doors fit for a king was the owner himself.

A nervous jitter danced down her arms.

One of the doors opened inward. A butler uniformed in red and gold gave a slight bow. His perfect posture made her want to stand up straighter. "Miss Presley, Prince Aleksandre will see you now."

Sara started to follow the man, then stopped. "Prince? As in a real prince?"

The butler inclined his head. "But of course." He motioned her forward with one hand. "If you please. His Majesty is waiting."

His Majesty? Oh my gosh. She was in a real castle with a real prince. Wait until Penny heard about this!

Knees quivering and curiosity driving her, Sara stepped into the room—a very large, regal office—and got her first glimpse of her benefactor.

The dark-haired man was standing with his back to her, gazing out at a panorama of green land and aqua sea. Legs spread, hands clasped at his back below a trim waist, his posture was as stiff as the butler's, his shoulders wide and exuding strength. Though he didn't appear much older than herself, an air of authority and power emanated from him. Dressed in a perfectly tailored suit, something about his well-honed physique looked eerily familiar.

The butler cleared his throat. If such a thing was possible, the servant's carriage grew more erect and perfect as he snapped to attention. "Your Majesty, may I present Miss

Sara Presley. Miss Presley, His Majesty Prince Aleksandre d'Gabriel."

The name struck a chord of alarm in Sara as the prince turned and leveled an empty stare in her direction.

"So Sara," he said quietly. "We meet again."

# CHAPTER TWO

"ALEKS!"

The woman before him clutched her chest, her mouth open in shock. She had gone as white and still as the alabaster statues lining the palace staircase. Aleks fought down the unexpected and disturbing urge to cross the Persian rug, take her in his arms and offer reassurance. Only the stern mental reminder of her ruthlessness kept him standing rigidly behind his desk, his heart thundering in his chest. Though he had once loved her enough to give up anything to have her, that love had long since turned to loathing. She was here for one reason and one reason only. Nico.

"You are surprised to see me." The sentence was a statement. He knew she'd be surprised. A surprise attack on one's enemies always worked best.

"Aleks," she said again and started toward him, one hand extended.

Aleks braced himself. Was that hope flaring in her sea-colored eyes?

He took a step back and forced a dark and forbidding expression. The woman paused. Her hand fell to her side. She looked lost and uncertain, and Aleks again fought the need to comfort her.

She was as beautiful to him now as she had been before, but he noted a subtle change, as well. The light had gone out in her. Where before she'd been vibrant and joyous, she now appeared older…sadder. Regret perhaps? Guilt? Or had life been unkind to Sara Presley?

He'd thought the terrors of war and near death added to the years of loathing had hardened him enough to face her. But he knew without a doubt he could not let her touch him. At least not now while his insides canted toward her like a seasick sailor.

"Welcome to Castle-by-the-Sea," he said. "I trust your accommodations are satisfactory."

Sara's look of bewilderment was exactly what he'd hoped. He'd caught her completely off guard.

"You're a prince?"

He inclined his head. "Ruler of Carvainia."

It was imperative she understand his power and place and forget about the lovesick youth he'd once been. He must be in control, and now that he'd seen her again, this was going to be more difficult than he'd thought.

"You never told me," she said. One hand went to her forehead and then fell to her side. "Why didn't you tell me?"

Considering her cruel abandonment, he was glad he hadn't. "Would it have made any difference?"

"No, of course not, but—"

He didn't believe her. "My country has enemies. To protect my friends and myself, I chose to attend college without fanfare, though I always had bodyguards at hand."

"You did?"

She seemed genuinely stunned by his royalty. Would she have been less treacherous, less likely to abandon him and his son if she had known the truth? Or would she have used the information to her advantage? "Remember Carlo and Stephan?"

"I thought they were students like you. Friends from your country."

"They were both." The knot in his stomach twisted. Though the difference in stations had separated them to some degree, he and his bodyguards were friends, as well. And Carlo had paid the ultimate price for his loyalty.

Sara Presley, the woman who held Nico's life in her unsuspecting hands, shook her head. Hair the color of cinnamon rustled against the shoulders of a simple yellow sundress— a dress that rose and fell with the rapid in and out of her anxious breathing.

"I don't understand." The tip of her tongue flicked out to moisten peach-colored lips. Aleks averted his gaze. No doubt her mouth had gone as dry as his, though for far different reasons. "What is this all about, Aleks? Why am I here?"

Though he felt no humor whatsoever, he offered an amused tilt of his head. "You are our grand prize winner. Remember?"

She scoffed. "Don't give me that. Something else is going on here."

He was not quite ready to reveal everything. "Sit down please. You seem…disturbed."

"Disturbed? I've never been so confused in my life. You disappeared five years ago and now suddenly I'm whisked out of my bookstore and into a castle. *Your* castle. And I didn't even know you *had* a castle. After all this time, I never expected to see you again."

He could believe that. If not for Nico, she wouldn't have. He almost said as much but knew he must be careful. His son's future rested with this woman. He must proceed with great caution. The battle plan was working well so far. He must not become reckless like a new recruit and ruin everything.

Sara moved to the chair he indicated, and he noticed the

slightest tremor in the hands she placed on the armrests. He turned his attention to her face. Even there he saw again the vulnerability. She was nervous and uncertain…and perhaps a bit scared. She was angry, too, though she had no right to be, all things considered.

She reached for her earring—a long chain of silver—and her fingers trembled. They were cold, too, he was certain, for he remembered the subtle nuances of her emotions. He didn't need to touch her to know she was anxious, maybe even afraid. Memories of her had tortured him enough.

He hardened his heart. Any weakness she displayed would be used to his advantage.

"If you think I've brought you here because I couldn't bear to be without you any longer, think again."

A deep rose color flushed her pale skin. "After what you did, that much is a mercy."

After what he'd done? "I don't equate a white lie about my royalty with outright betrayal, particularly when that white lie was intended to protect all concerned."

Eyelashes as lush as sable blinked at him. "I have no idea what you're talking about."

He quelled the memory of his lips against those eyelids and the feel of her lashes tickling his skin. "Oh, I think you do."

Her chin hitched up. "No, I don't. All I know was that your father fell ill and you had to return home. You promised to be in touch, but I never heard from you again."

Had he not known the lengths to which his mother had gone to contact this woman, he would have believed her lies.

"Nor did I hear from you."

*You didn't even bother to contact me about the child you were carrying. My child.* But he left those last words unspoken. He would let her lies continue while she backed herself into a corner. Then, when she met Nico, she would be forced to admit her transgression and agree to his demands.

"How could I contact you? You weren't even honest enough to tell me who you were or where you lived. I thought you lived in Italy. I thought your name was Aleks Gabriel."

He stepped down from the raised dais where his desk was situated. "Enough!"

"Don't 'enough' me, Mr. Prince. I'm not one of your subjects. I demand to know what's going on. Why the outlandish ruse to get me here?"

"Ruse?"

"Don't play dumb. I didn't win any all-expense-paid vacation to a health spa."

"Are you certain of that? Have you not been treated well by my staff? Did the masseuse and hairdresser not visit your rooms? Do you not have a personal attendant at your beck and call?"

"Well, yes, but…"

"And this treatment shall continue for the duration of your stay. Whatever you need is at your disposal."

She blinked again, confusion warring with the need to assert herself. Aleks felt victory at hand. A confused enemy was easy to defeat.

Feeling in total control now, his emotions ruthlessly in check, he moved to her side and reached for her hand. The skin was incredibly soft and silken and every bit as cold as he'd known it would be. As cold as her soul.

Sara snatched her hand away and glared at him.

Teeth tight, he took her elbow and forced her to stand. "Come. I want you to meet someone."

"Who?" She tried to pull away again but Aleks held tight to her arm, propelling her to the door.

"I think," he said through gritted teeth, "you will be greatly surprised."

Sara's knees trembled as Aleks's strong fingers dug into her skin. She recalled all the times he'd placed his hand exactly there, guiding her with such courtesy and grace across campus, into a movie or a restaurant, into a car. But today, his hold was impersonal, even cruel.

Her head spun with the impact of the last few minutes. She could hardly take everything in. For a brief moment, she had entertained the hope that Aleks had brought her here to set the past straight. As furious as she was that he would contact her now when it was too late, and as much as she wanted to hate him for all the anguish she had gone through, Sara could not deny that she was still very much attracted to the man who even now rushed her past stiff-backed guards, over marbled floors and down a furnished hallway to an elevator.

Everyone they passed stopped working to pay respects to their ruler, and Sara felt the curious stares of each one fall on her, as well.

Saints alive, the man who'd left her pregnant and penniless was a prince. She couldn't take it in. Her Aleks, the man she'd loved, the man she'd given her innocence to, was a wealthy, powerful prince. He could have easily cared for her and their baby even if he had no longer wanted her. Surely, he would have wanted his son.

Why, oh, why had he left without a word?

The bitter taste of gall rose in her throat. It was too late now. Her baby was gone and Aleks would never know what he'd thrown away. Her stomach rolled with nerves and fear and loss. She wanted to stop at a restroom and throw up.

But Aleks seemed mercilessly unaware of her distress as he thrust her into a gleaming brass-and-mirrored elevator. The door pinged shut and he loosened his grip to push a number.

She'd dreamed of him for so long and now here he was, in the flesh. But oh, that flesh was hard and unyielding, not warm and loving as she remembered.

He loathed her. That much was evident. But why? He was the one who'd abandoned her.

She longed to ask, but right now she was still in shock and if she admitted it, more than a little unnerved. Something was very wrong here and until she understood, she would play her hand very close to the vest.

During the entire elevator ride, Aleks stared straight ahead at the closed doors, avoiding eye contact, and said not a word. He was as stiff and cold as an icicle but still as handsome and dynamic as ever.

But the years had altered him. Where he'd been a charming, carefree college student, engrossed in getting his master's degree while embracing sports and cars and the American college life, today he was a solemn man with hard eyes.

He was so near, this man who'd broken her heart that she could feel the tension in his frame and smell the fabric of his navy blue jacket. But he was also as far away as her bookstore.

She should be demanding her release, filing a kidnapping complaint, or at the least, slapping his royal face. But here she was noticing the added lines around his mouth, his beautiful, dark skin, and remembering the time he'd buried them in autumn leaves and they'd kissed and cuddled in their leafy hideaway, content to be together and so completely in love.

Or at least, she had been.

"I never knew you at all, did I?" she whispered, surprised that she had spoken aloud.

Aleks slowly turned his head and stared at her with those icy eyes. "Ours was a brief romance. A fling I think you Americans call it."

A fling. The word seared her heart like a hot iron against tender flesh. She'd given him everything she had to give. And he called their love a fling.

How could she have fallen for a man who had deceived her so badly? He had not only walked out with little explanation but he'd never been honest with her from the beginning.

He was a royal prince, but she was a royal fool.

The elevator eased to a stop and the doors slid open. Aleks stepped aside, holding the door with one hand while motioning with the other for her to exit. She did so, her mind reeling.

Who could he possibly want her to meet? Why was she here? And why didn't he just tell her what was going on?

The floor they stepped out on was similar to the one where her suite of rooms was situated. A long, carpeted hallway lit by sconces and new lighting—a fascinating mix of old and modern—was guarded by a pair of uniformed men. Stunning murals graced the vaulted ceilings. Tapestry and gilded paintings lined the walls above elegant furniture groupings. At one end an arched window looked out at the sunlit day. Sara had never seen a place of such over-the-top wealth and splendor.

Aleks seemed impervious to it all as he reclaimed her elbow.

Two people, a man and a woman both dressed in white uniforms, sat outside a closed door but quickly stood to attention when they saw Aleks approach. They turned curious gazes in Sara's direction.

Aleks glanced toward the closed door. The cold mask

slipped from his face. For the briefest moment, Sara was certain she saw tenderness…and fear.

"How is he?"

Something in his voice gave Sara pause. She stared at the side of his face, trying to comprehend the undercurrent flowing between him and the others.

"He's sleeping, Your Majesty."

The news seemed to bring relief to Aleks. Some of the tension flowed out of him.

"Excellent." He occasioned a glance at Sara. The frosty glare was back. "We will go inside."

Whoever resided inside that room held special meaning to the Prince of Carvainia. But what did this have to do with her?

"Who—" she started, but Aleks shot her a warning glance as if daring her to make a noise and wake the sleeper. Sara fell silent.

He pushed the door open. Sara's pulse rate elevated with an inexplicable nervousness as they tiptoed inside.

Sara's first impression was a smell. Though the overriding scent was antiseptic, another odor that she couldn't quite place lingered, too. This was a medical ward, not a bedroom.

The large room was semidarkened with enough light to see and work by but not enough to disturb the sleeper. An array of medical equipment looked out of place next to a stunning iron bed canopied in blood-red draperies trimmed in gold and black. The quiet was broken only by the *shoosh* and *burr* of those machines.

At the sight of Aleks, the attendants hovering near the bed bowed and backed silently away, but not before their eyes flicked over Sara, all with the same identical and troubling expression. Sara's nervousness increased. Her palms began to sweat.

Following Aleks's lead, she approached the enormous, raised bed.

A handsome little boy rested against the pillows, his long eyelashes startling black against his pale cheeks. He was thin and his skin color was an odd gold-over-olive. The scent she'd noticed rose from the bed, the odor of fever.

"Is he sick?" she whispered.

A muscle jerked in Aleks's cheek. "Very."

"Poor little child. I'm so sorry."

Aleks gave her a strange look. "As am I."

They stood in silence, staring down at the sleeping child. Looking at the small boy was a powerful reminder and Sara ached both for him and for herself. Her child would have been near the age of this little boy. She prayed that wherever he was, her son was well and that no sickness ever befell him.

"What's wrong with him?"

"A virus has attacked his liver."

"Will he be all right?"

Aleks glared at her, his expression so bewildering and strange that she grew afraid.

"We will know soon."

A sense of silent anticipation hovered in the room as if the people standing in the shadows held their collective breath.

"Who is he?" she whispered.

The mask of coldness seemed to slip for a moment, and Sara could have sworn he was hurting. "He is my son."

"Your...son?" The words nearly choked her.

She placed a hand over her womb. She felt so empty. Aleks had moved on without a backward glance, marrying and producing a son. He had a child. She had nothing but an empty ache.

Did her little boy, wherever he was, look like this? Did he have Aleks's black eyelashes and aristocratic nose?

Against the lump of regret and longing that clogged her throat, she said, "Your son is very beautiful. He deserves to be well."

Aleks took both her elbows and turned her to face him. He stared at her long and hard and without mercy. She swallowed, the sound loud in a room where only the breath of a small boy and his incessant machinery broke the silence.

His fingers tightened. "So does yours."

She frowned, puzzled. An erratic beat of something she couldn't name started deep inside, shouting a warning that she did not comprehend.

"My son?" she asked, voice trembling with dread. "What do you mean?" And how did he know? How could he possibly know about her son? About their son?

Aleks's black eyes held hers as if peering into her soul. Then slowly, slowly, they slid away to the sleeping child.

In a voice of ice and steel, he said, "Meet Nico, or as he is officially known, Crown Prince Domenico Emmanuel Lucian d'Gabriel…the child you abandoned."

Every ounce of strength left Sara's body. Her knees buckled. And the world went black.

# CHAPTER THREE

PRINCE ALEKSANDRE STOOD beside Sara's bed waiting for her to regain consciousness. The fainting spell had come as a surprise. One minute she'd been staring at him in horror and the next she'd crumpled like tissue paper.

He was still pondering the meaning of her reaction.

In an effort not to disturb Nico, he'd swept her into his arms and carried her here to the guest wing. Halfway to the suite, he'd been tempted to hand her off to one of the guards trailing them. Not because she was too heavy. She weighed nothing. But because the feel of her curves pressed against him stirred more than memories.

Now as he glared down at her, willing her to awaken, he couldn't help noticing the way her red hair spilled over the white pillow like fire on snow. Nor could he miss the gentle curve of her mouth or the tiny scar above her lip that he'd once found particularly tasty.

She moaned softly. He steeled himself with a stern reminder than his attraction to this woman had already cost him enough.

She opened her eyes and looked around, her expression clouded. He waited, silent while she regained her bearings.

With a gasp of awareness, she sat up.

Aleks pressed her back. "Lie still. You've had a shock."

She slapped at him. "Get your hands off me."

In a flurry of movement the two bodyguards flanked him, hands on their weapons. He waved them off. "Leave us."

"But Your Majesty—"

"Leave us. This woman poses no threat." At least not physically.

Sara swung her legs over the side of the bed and stood. "That's what you think."

Had this been another woman or another time, Aleks would have laughed. Sara barely came to his chin and even with fists tight at her sides and eyes shooting sparks, she was no match for his size and strength.

The guards looked from Sara to Aleks, ever vigilant, but they followed his command and backed from the room. He knew very well they were both standing with ears pressed against the closed door, anxious because he was out of their sight with a fiery woman.

The moment they disappeared, Sara stormed toward him, long hair flying wildly around her shoulders. "Is Nico my son? Are you telling me the truth?"

"Nico is *my* son and mine alone. You gave him away."

All of the fight went out of her. Her shoulders slumped. She pressed both hands to her stomach and bent forward so that Aleks wondered if she might faint again. He started to her but stopped when she groaned. "Oh, God, I did. I gave him away."

This was the truth he'd dreaded hearing but the truth as he already knew it. Though he'd loved this woman, he'd never really known what she was capable of until she had abandoned their child.

"Did you hate me that much, Sara?"

He hadn't intended to ask the question nor to sound quite as vulnerable as he feared he did.

"I never hated you, Aleks. I loved you." Disturbingly haunted eyes implored him. "I longed for you."

He glanced away. "You will forgive me if I don't believe that."

"You promised to come back. I waited."

His lips curled in distaste. "Not for long."

"I was pregnant with your child, alone, scared out of my mind, with no means of support. What was I supposed to do?"

*Not sell my son to the highest bidder*, he thought. If not for the queen's intervention, someone else would have paid the price for the handsome male child with royal bloodlines, though another family would not have known the boy was a crown prince, and the prince of Carvainia would never have had a son and an heir. The fury of that near disaster raced through his blood with the sting of alcohol on an open wound.

Seething, he turned his back to stare blindly at a dressing table littered with feminine jars and a silver hand mirror. "The past does not matter to me. *You* do not matter to me."

"Then why did you bring me here after all this time? To punish me? To let me know how much you despise me for putting our son up for adoption?"

"I never wanted you involved in his life. Let me make that clear." Slowly, he pivoted, jaw tight enough to crack a bone. "You are here because I had no other choice."

She didn't need to know about the stir her presence had caused, both among the staff and within the royal family. As it was, the queen had taken to her bed with a migraine the moment Sara Presley entered the castle. He regretted that deeply.

Without his mother's help and guidance during that terrible time five years ago, he wasn't sure he could have survived. First, he'd lost his father. Then an old enemy, the greedy king of Perseidia had perceived a weakness in the new Carvainian government and had invaded their northern borders. Like the warriors of old and as he'd been trained, he'd led his men into battle and had come out the victor. But at what price? Wounded, and heartsick at the loss of fine young men, he'd been further shattered by the news that his former love had given birth to his son and was offering the baby to the highest bidder.

Though the queen had expressed serious doubt, Aleks was convinced the child was his. Sara had been an innocent when they'd first come together, so shy and eager and loving. He could not imagine her with another man.

She'd likely had several men by now, but he refused to care.

"How did you learn about the baby?" she asked. "How did he get here?"

"Money and power have their advantages."

"Why didn't you contact me? Where were you?"

"At war, fighting for my country's independence where I belonged." He chopped the air in impatience. "None of this matters anymore, Sara."

"It matters to me! I've missed four years of my baby's life, four years of wondering if the wealthy family that adopted him loves him, wondering if he's all right. Then suddenly I'm whisked away from America without explanation to discover he's been here with you all along. Why have you contacted me now when you didn't then?"

Aleks grabbed her arm and stared down into her face with all the will he had inside him.

"Let me explain as clearly as I know how." He swallowed, hating the words to come. "Nico…is dying."

"No!" Sara shrank away from him, a hand to her throat. "Please no."

The stark despair in her expression would have shaken

him had he not been braced for it. She had ignored her child since birth. A pained cry and a few tears would not convince him that she cared.

"His only hope is a liver transplant."

Sara slid onto a chair and buried her face in her hands. Once again, Aleks battled back an urge to go to her. He stood with rigid military discipline, reminding himself that this woman was the enemy. This woman had no scruples. This woman had tossed his child away like a stray dog.

When she lifted her tearstained face, his gut spasmed. She'd looked this way on the day he'd gotten news that his father was dying. She'd cried for him.

He'd been a fool then. He wouldn't be again.

"Is he on a transplant list?" she asked. "I don't know how things like that work here in your country. What can be done?"

"The best hope for Nico is a living donor. His body would then regenerate the donated segment into a full-sized body part while the donor's body would also fully recover. But Carvainia is a country of genetically similar people. No one we can find shares his blood type."

"AB negative," she murmured.

"Yours, I assume."

She nodded. "Yes."

"Nor does anyone, including myself, my mother, nor any of the royal family share the specific blood markers that he requires." Impatient, he chopped the air again. "I don't pretend to understand the medical details. I only know that Nico is dying and his only hope is a living donor who matches him as exactly as possible."

Perched on the edge of the chair, she bent forward, forearms against her thighs, hair falling over her shoulders as she looked up. "And that's why I'm here, isn't it? To be his donor."

Aleks tensed. His heart galloped in his chest like one of his racehorses. If he was to gain Sara's cooperation, he must proceed with extreme caution.

"You needn't worry. I will pay you well."

A soft gasp escaped her. "You'll...pay me?"

Though she sounded less than eager, Aleks was confident she would agree once she understood the terms. Greed was a powerful incentive. A baby, a body part, it was all the same to a woman like Sara. "One million American dollars."

Something hard shifted through her features. "No."

Aleks blinked once, slowly, certain he had heard wrong. "No?"

Her lips tightened. "I said no."

Sickness churned in his belly, and for the first time, he began to doubt his plan. What if he failed? What if Sara Presley was even more heartless than he'd expected?

The muscles in his neck tightened to the breaking point. "Then name your price. Whatever you want is yours."

Sara stared back at him with eyes that had turned the color of a stormy sea. They were eyes that had beguiled him when he was young and foolish. Eyes that had promised so much and then had forgotten him. Eyes that now defied him.

With a near-regal grace, she rose, fists clenched at her side, her chin thrust upward. "Then here's the deal, Prince Charming. I want to spend time with my son and get to know him. I want to be his mother."

She wanted to be Nico's mother? Cold fear sliced through Aleks. "You should have thought about that a long time ago, Sara. Nico is mine and mine alone. You will have no part in his life. None ever."

"A little late for that, don't you think? You've brought me here. I'm involved."

"As a hired body part. Nothing else."

She blanched and rocked back, biting down on her bottom lip.

Aleks refused to be moved by her wounded reaction. He would do anything to protect Nico, particularly from the woman who had abandoned them both.

In clipped tones with barely suppressed anger, he said, "Presenting a sick child with a long-lost mother is not in his best interest. Have you no compassion whatsoever? Think of the questions he'd ask! Do you want him to know that he was given away at birth? Do you want him asking why he's never known about you? His health is far too fragile for that kind of revelation."

Sara made a tiny noise of dismay and began to move around the room. She twisted her fingers together, worrying a small gold ring on her pinky. The hem of the yellow sundress swished softly against her thighs as curvy hips swayed below a slender waist.

Aleks didn't want to notice her lush body or to remember the silk of her thighs against his palms. With firm resolve, he focused on the coldness of her heart and on his plan.

Now, while Sara was still in a state of shock, he had to press his advantage. "I'm prepared to pay you a million if you are a match and another million after the surgery."

He was prepared to pay her far more than that should she balk. Everyone had a price.

Like a wounded tigress, Sara whirled on him. "Get this through your pig head, Aleks. I don't want your money. I want my child."

"He is not yours to want."

On a sharp inhale, she drew up to her full height, shoulders high and tight as she contemplated him.

While Aleks held his own breath, she exhaled in a rush of words. "Then I won't cooperate. You'll have to search elsewhere for your donor." She marched to the door and yanked it open. "You'll also have to excuse me, *Your Majesty*, I must pack. I'm leaving in the morning."

Aleks was stunned by the woman's audacity. She was showing him out?

When he didn't move, she said, "I never had the chance to know my son. I don't want your money. I want to spend time with Nico. That's the deal, Aleks. Take it, or I'm going home."

Aleks could scarcely believe this was happening. She was bargaining with Nico's life. But why? He didn't believe for one second that she would turn down a million dollars in the end. Why the pretense of belated maternal feelings? Did she despise him enough to hurt him through Nico?

Whatever the reason, Sara was worse than he'd dreamed.

"Close the door."

He had no wish for this conversation to be carried by the servants to his mother's ears. She was upset enough. She would be livid to learn of the bargain he was about to strike.

The door snapped shut. Sara stood with one hand on the pull, facing him as calmly as if they were trading automobiles. Only the quiver of pulse above her collarbone indicated distress. "Do we have a deal?"

What choice did he have? He wanted Nico alive and well, and Sara was his only chance.

"You may visit his rooms, but either I or the queen must be present at all times."

She cocked her head. A silver earring glinted against the pale skin of her neck. "You don't trust me."

About as much as he trusted the king of Perseidia. "Not in the least."

A small skirmish went on behind sea-blue eyes but finally she said, "Okay, agreed, as long as I can see him as often as I like."

"Done." He reached for the door handle and paused. "One thing, though, Sara, is not negotiable."

She regarded him warily. "And that is?"

Calling upon four years of festered anger and bitterness, he said, "Nico is never to know you are the bitch that whelped him."

The color, which had drained from her face, now surged forth, setting her delicate skin aflame. She raised a hand as if to strike him. He caught her wrist. "I think not."

Long after Aleks left her alone, Sara sat at the window staring out at the magical country of Carvainia. Aleks's country. Her baby's country.

Emotional exhaustion made her limbs heavy so she could hardly lift her hands to swipe at the tears flowing down her cheeks.

Her baby was here. After the years of guilt and regret, she'd found him. All this time of worry and he'd been right here with his natural father. She was glad for that, though still astonished by the turn of events. Nothing Aleks said in explanation had made any sense. He claimed to have contacted her but she knew he hadn't. And yet, how could he have known about the pregnancy? How could he have gotten custody of Nico?

Joy at finding her son intermingled with the loss of years and the fear that he was deathly ill. Now that she'd found him again, she couldn't bear the thought of losing him.

She longed to go to his rooms and stay with him every minute of every day. But she knew without a doubt that if she tried to see him now, without Aleks's permission, a host of staff would block her way.

And so she waited for him to return with the contract he

insisted she sign. A contract. Dear heaven. What had happened to the man who'd claimed to love her?

She reached for a tissue and rubbed at eyes gone raw and hot. A sob slipped from her lips. Aleks had offered her money to help her own child. How low she had fallen in his eyes that he would believe such an offer was necessary. She would do anything to see Nico well. Her demands to see him were nothing more than a bluff though she'd been praying the entire time that Aleks would fall for it. Even if he'd refused, she would never have left this castle without doing all in her power to save her child's life.

Part of her didn't blame Aleks for despising her. Didn't she despise herself for letting go when she might have found a way to keep their child? Wasn't she haunted by a host of what-might-have-beens?

The door opened and Antonia entered carrying a tray. "You must eat something, Miss Sara. Lunch is long past."

The young woman set the tray on the small round table at Sara's elbow. Sara took one glance at the array of beautifully prepared finger foods and shook her head. "Thank you, Antonia. I'm not hungry."

Antonia studied her with compassion. "You are upset, miss. Let me get some cucumber slices for the swelling in your eyes. And perhaps I could arrange a soothing massage and a spa treatment?"

Sara shook her head. No amount of pampering could soothe the ache in her heart. "Not now."

Clearly wishing to provide service, but at a loss, Antonia lingered. Except for the attendant's fidgety movements the suite was quiet, the sounds of activity outside the door silenced by the thick stone walls.

"A refreshing candle, then," Antonia said.

The rasp of match against striker sawed at Sara's raw nerve endings. A teardrop flame flared, and then the smell of sulfur mingled with the clean scent of vanilla.

"If you are certain you don't require anything—"

"Nothing." Sara lifted a limp hand, but the effort was too much and she let it fall to her lap. "Thanks."

"If you should change your mind, please ring. Prince Aleksandre left specific orders that you are to have everything you desire."

Yeah, right, anything but her son. Sara gave a short, joyless laugh. "Your Prince Aleksandre is a royal jerk."

Antonia gasped and with a polite bow made a hasty exit, apparently disturbed that anyone would speak ill of the prince. Sara supposed she should be more careful. After all, this was not America. For all she knew, she may have just committed a crime punishable by stoning.

No, Aleks wouldn't hurt her. She knew that for certain, not because of the love they'd once shared, but because he needed her.

She reached for a strawberry but didn't eat it. How could she eat with this enormous wad of hope and fear and longing filling up her insides? When she could touch her son and hear his voice and see him smile, then she would be filled in a way that had nothing to do with food.

If only Aleks would hurry, but she knew he would not. He was no longer the kind and playful and fiercely protective man she remembered. He was a ruling prince, unyielding and cold. Perhaps the war had done that to him. She'd been shocked to hear that he'd fought beside his men, and yet her Aleks would have done exactly that.

*Her* Aleks. A bitter laugh escaped her, sounding loud in the large, quiet room. This Prince Aleksandre was not her Aleks.

Her Aleks had loved her, and she had loved him.

But she had to face the truth and her own culpability. She had killed his love by putting his son up for adoption.

She picked at the strawberry's leafy cap.

A new fear crowded into an already overwhelmed mind.

Aleks had agreed to let her spend time with Nico now. But what would happen after the surgery, after Nico was well again?

Aleksandre d'Gabriel was the absolute law and ruler of Carvainia. She, a simple bookshop owner from Kansas, had no legal rights in this place. Once Aleks had what he wanted from her, would she ever see her son again?

# CHAPTER FOUR

SARA SAT ON A PLUSH CHAIR at Nico's bedside, waiting for her son to awaken. After two impatient hours with the doctors and a miserable thirty minutes hashing over the details of Aleks's contract, she'd insisted on coming to Nico's room.

"He sleeps most of the time," Aleks had said, obviously trying to forestall her visit.

She'd hitched her stubborn chin. "Then I will watch him sleep."

"I have a nation to run."

After four years and thousands of miles, Sara was not about to let Aleks's reluctance keep her away from her baby. He'd promised and he would deliver.

"The decision to be present was yours."

Finally, he'd conceded and escorted her to this wing, which Sara understood to be a medical floor fully staffed for the royal family.

Both thrilled and terrified, but utterly determined to make up for lost time, she gazed at the sleeping baby face and waited. She may have appeared calm with her hands resting serenely in her lap, but her heart hammered and she could barely breathe.

The tension was magnified by the imposing ruler who stood like a stone sentry at the foot of Nico's bed. Sara's gaze flicked briefly to him. Jaw rigid, Aleks never even glanced her way. He treated her with cold courtesy and little else. She was grateful that his staff was more inclined toward friendliness. Though none of them voiced their knowledge of her unique situation, she was certain they at least suspected the reasons for her presence. Antonia knew Sara was the hoped-for organ donor. Beyond that, Sara had no idea what Aleks had told his employees about her.

Having only seen Nico briefly at birth, it was surreal to realize this was the baby she'd carried beneath her heart, the baby she'd mourned and hunted and prayed for. Over the years, she'd imagined what he would look like. She'd dreamed of finding him again, certain she would recognize her own son. She wouldn't have. He was all Aleks and nothing of her.

And yet he was everything she'd dreamed and more.

At a movement from the pillows, Sara's heart, already pounding out of her chest, galloped even harder. He was waking. She would meet him. Finally. She pressed her hands into her knees to keep from leaping from the chair and rushing forward.

Nico's thick lashes fluttered upward. Glazed, feverish eyes locked on the man at the end of the bed. His thin face brightened. "Papa."

That one small, breathy word held such power. Sara's whole being heaved toward the sick child. And the hard and mighty ruler of Carvainia melted like butter left too long in the sun.

Aleks tweaked the boy's sheet-covered toe. "Ah, the great and lazy Prince Nico has awakened."

The joke must have been a familiar one for the child offered a feeble grin, his sick eyes twinkling. "A growing boy needs his rest."

Aleks laughed softly. "Indeed. A growing boy also needs food. Maria tells me you refused your meal."

"Food tastes nasty, Papa." His tone apologized as though he was aware of his father's worry and sad to make it worse.

Aleks moved to the boy's side. "I know, son, but you must try." He touched Nico's cheek. "Promise Papa you will try."

Sara shared the pleading despair in Aleks's voice. Nico was far too thin. His arms, resting along the sides of his body on top of the damask coverlet, were like sticks and his cheekbones stood out above the hollows of his face.

The small handsome head nodded. His tongue flicked over dry lips. "I promise."

Carefully perching on the bed's edge so that the mattress barely shifted, Aleks reached for a glass of water. "Have a drink for Papa."

Gently cradling Nico's head, the prince raised the boy enough for a few sips. Then he brushed a hand over Nico's temple, smoothing bed-tumbled hair. "Do you feel like playing a game?"

"I'm a bit tired, Papa." For indeed, he seemed to have expended all his energy on a simple drink of water.

Aleks's chest rose and fell in a heavy sigh. He patted the child's fragile chest and sat back in the chair, shoulders angled toward Sara. Her pulse leaped.

"I don't want to tire him," she murmured through dry lips. Her son was desperately ill and conversation took so much out of his frail body.

Aleks's gaze, so warm and tender with Nico, frosted over. "Come."

As she stood, her knees trembled in tandem with her emotions. "Maybe we should do this later. I'm content to watch him sleep."

His Majesty didn't look as though he bought that. He turned back to the boy. "Someone has come to say hello."

Sara stepped closer and with the movement brushed Aleks's knees. Once upon a time he would have pulled her onto his lap, and she would have gone willingly for kisses and laughter. Today, he shifted away as though her touch was poison. Shoulders tense and mouth grim, animosity flowed from him. Surely, Nico would feel the tension and be put off by it.

She longed to touch him, both of them, and to make them understand how sorry she was for everything. She'd made a terrible mistake in letting Nico go, but she'd also paid a terrible price. Couldn't Aleks see that? She'd lost everything that mattered—him, her baby.

The beautiful little prince was flesh of her flesh and yet she did not know him at all. The pain of that truth would burn forever.

"Hello, Nico," she said, amazed to sound so normal. "My name is Sara. I'm—"

As though afraid of what she'd say, Aleks interrupted. "Sara is someone I knew in America."

Nico's dark eyes swung up to hers. "You were my father's friend at university?"

So sweet. So innocent. So unaware of the painful alliance between his father and herself.

A lump formed in her throat. She cleared it. "Yes."

"Papa, did you tell me about Sara? I don't remember her in your stories."

Aleks shifted uncomfortably, but he kept his tone light. "Remember the girl who capsized the boat and dumped me into the river?"

Sara stared at him, stunned. He'd spoken of her to Nico? But Aleks's expression was as hard as his jaw. If he remembered the time fondly, he wasn't about to let her know.

Nico giggled. "That was you?"

"Yes, that was me," she said, delighted to have found common ground. "I wasn't the best swimmer."

"And Papa had to save you." Nico's voice was weak, but he seemed to relish casting his father as a hero.

"Yes. You should have seen him. We were both laughing so hard, I think I nearly drowned him."

"Papa said you spilled the picnic basket, too."

"I'm afraid so. Your poor Papa went without lunch except for the chocolate bar we shared."

They'd shared a great deal more than chocolate that weekend. A master boatman, Aleks had wanted to canoe the mighty Mississippi River, so they'd driven to St. Louis for the day and wound up spending the weekend. Sara had often wondered if she'd gotten pregnant during those magical two days before Aleks suddenly and completely disappeared from her life.

Overtaken by nostalgia, she turned to look at Aleks.

Abruptly he pushed up from the bed's edge and stepped away. "This little trip down memory lane has been fun, but I think we should let Nico rest now."

The interruption shouldn't have come as a surprise, but it did sting. That Aleks despised her and any memory of their time together was painfully clear.

But he was also correct. The boy was visibly fading. With no forethought, Sara touched Nico's forehead. He was too warm, but touching him was a salve for her soul. This was her baby. Her son! She couldn't get over the thrill of it.

"Your Papa is right. You must rest and get well so you can someday have your own wonderful adventures."

Nico's eyelids drooped but he struggled to keep them open.

"Will you be here after my nap? And tell me about America? Papa liked America very much."

Sara looked to the man in charge and held his frigid gaze in challenge. If his feelings about America had anything to do with her, she would never know. "I will be back, Nico. I promise."

Aleks glared at her for one long moment, then bent low to kiss the boy's forehead and softly murmur something. By the time he straightened, Nico's eyes were closed.

Still the ruler prince did not move. He stared into the face of his son with an expression of love and sorrow and longing.

Prince Aleksandre loved their son. There was no denying that.

What he didn't understand was that she loved him, too. And she would do anything, even die on the operating table, to make him well.

She glanced at the stiff-backed man who'd broken her heart, and remembered a time she would have done the same for him.

And yet, to him, she'd been nothing more than a fling.

Without a doubt the day of Nico's surgery was the hardest day of Aleks's life, harder even than the day he'd been wounded and nearly died, harder than the day word had come of Sara's betrayal. Every dream and hope of the future hinged on the outcome of today's surgery.

Twice he had gone down to his office, but his mind refused to think about anything except the transplant taking place here in the especially constructed surgical wing of the castle. For once, duty to his country took second place.

He gazed at the unconscious Sara Presley, her surgery complete. He didn't know why he'd come here to the recovery suite to see her. Gratitude, he supposed.

She'd kept her promises thus far though she'd driven him to distraction with her demands to see Nico. He was trapped by his own design, a poor tactic that put him in frequent contact with the enemy of his heart. Regardless of his oath to ignore her, she'd been on his mind constantly and in his presence so often that her subtle perfume seemed to linger in his nostrils long after they parted.

Queen Irena was utterly terrified of this American. Perhaps he was, too, though for different reasons.

With tubes running from her body and her lips swollen, Sara Presley looked fragile, vulnerable and utterly alone. Other than some distant relatives, she had no real family to rally round her. According to his staff, she had friends in Kansas, in particular a co-owner of a book store who she telephoned frequently, but here she was alone. Alone and at his mercy.

He'd expected to revel in the victory, but instead, he felt the troubling urge to comfort her. It was an urge he'd battled from the moment she'd entered his world a week ago, full of fire and fury and lies. He clenched his fists at his sides. It was the lies that kept him from touching her.

He knew what she'd done. No amount of talking would change it.

"When can she return to America?" Queen Irena had asked the moment Sara was wheeled out of the operating room.

"She has done us no harm, Mother," he'd answered, too weary and worried to dwell on the dangers the American woman presented. Today she brought only good.

"But she could at any time. She is not to be trusted."

How well he knew.

To make matters worse, in the days leading up to the surgery, Sara had hardly left Nico's bedside. She'd read to him, played quiet games or, most often, simply sat at his side watching while he slept. More than once, Aleks had been forced by his own unsettled emotions to leave the room, something he'd sworn not to do.

The innocent, affectionate Nico had quickly—too quickly—come to welcome her company.

Aleks squeezed the bridge of his nose.

To this point, Nico accepted Sara's presence as a friend willing and able to help him get well. He was too small and too ill to understand more than that.

"Aleks." The word was a husky whisper that drew him back to Sara. Her puffy-lidded eyes were opened the slightest bit. She swallowed hard as though her throat was raw. It probably was. "Nico," she rasped. "Is Nico okay?"

"I'm still awaiting word."

Her head moved up and down once before she closed her eyes again. A nurse moved in to read the monitors. "Miss Presley, do you need something for the pain?"

Red hair swished against the stiff linen pillow. "Nico. Is Nico okay?"

The nurse looked to Aleks and he shook his head. "I'll let you know if she complains."

He didn't know why he'd said that. He had no intentions of remaining here with Sara.

The door to the room opened and Dr. Konstantine, attired in green operating scrubs, entered. Though specialists had done the transplant, the royal physician had been present at Aleksandre's request.

"I have news, Your Majesty."

Aleksandre spun to face him, gripping the bed rail in desperate hope. "How is he?"

The doctor's tired face wrinkled with a smile. "Exceptional. The transplant is complete, Prince Nico came through very well, and already the tiny liver has begun to function.

Barring unexpected complications, the prognosis, according to Dr. Schlessinger and all involved, is a full recovery and a long and healthy life."

An exultant cry of relieved joy rose in Aleks's throat. It was all he could do not to shout it out.

Behind him, a cold hand found his and squeezed. He looked back to see Sara, forehead wrinkled with emotion as tears flowed down her face.

He carefully slid his hand from beneath hers, but not before something strong and troubling bloomed in his chest.

Sara awoke to the sound of Nico's cries. Her side ached and she still felt as wobbly as a flat tire, but neither mattered at the moment.

Bracing her tender incision with one arm held tightly against her side, she slipped from the bed and hobbled, bent forward, across the dimly lit hallway. Her knees trembled from the effort.

She had no idea what time it was, but from the dark quiet, the hour must be late.

At Nico's doorway, an attendant blocked her entrance. "I'm sorry, Miss Presley, we have our orders."

She ground her teeth in frustration. How many times had she repeated this scenario in the last few days?

"He's crying. Please. He needs me."

"I cannot let you inside without the queen or His Majesty Prince Aleksandre."

"Then call one of them."

"It's midnight. They're asleep."

"Nico is not asleep. He's crying."

The attendant remained firm. "He has a nurse."

A nurse was not the same as a mother who adored him, whether the child knew her or not.

Sara tired to peer around him. "Who is the nurse?"

"Maria is with him tonight."

Maria. Regardless of her smiling face, the woman bothered Sara. Nonetheless, she could see the attendant was not going to give in, and there was little she could do until the morning.

A niggle of an idea came to her. Perhaps there *was* something she could do.

Heedless of her bare feet and nightgown, she hobbled to the elevator; leaned, breathless, against the interior; and rode up to the family wing. The floor was quiet and devoid of staff, lit only by sconces along each wall.

In the time she'd been in the castle, she'd learned the power of talking to the castle employees. Because of Antonia especially, Sara knew exactly which room belonged to Prince Aleksandre. Normally, Nico, too, slept in this wing, near his father.

Hurrying now, lest a security camera spot her, she made her way to the door and knocked softly.

"Aleks," she called. Annoyingly fatigued from the journey, her breath came in small puffs.

The door opened so quickly she could have sworn he'd been standing just inside. Yet, his disheveled appearance said he'd been asleep—and restless.

Sara's pulse skipped a beat.

Wearing only pajama bottoms, the prince looked as he had that one fabulous weekend long ago. Strong, masculine, and oh-so sexy.

She hadn't considered *this* before rushing up here.

Sara!" He ran splayed fingers over his head. "What are you doing?"

"Nico."

Suddenly coming to attention, he grasped her arm.

"What's wrong? Is he worse?"

"No, no. I don't know. They wouldn't let me in. I need to be with him. You promised—"

Eyes narrowing, Aleks yanked her closer. Her side ached but she hardly noticed. Aleks's naked chest was warm and muscular and brushing the front of her thin nightgown.

His Royal Majesty was unfazed. "Are you telling me that you've come up here to my room and awakened me, because you want to pay Nico a visit in the middle of the night?"

She tossed her chin up. "Yes."

In the dim lighting his black eyes glittered. "No. He has round-the-clock nurses. Isn't Maria with him?"

"I don't trust that woman."

Aleks scoffed.

"You have no idea what you're saying. Maria is a trusted and loyal friend. Her son died—" He stopped, pain flickering through his eyes. He pressed his lips into a line and glanced down the hallway before tugging on her arm. "Come inside. I do not want everyone in the palace gossiping about the two of us in our nightclothes. You've caused enough gossip already."

"I want to see my son."

Pulling her inside, he shut the door and snapped on a lamp. Though they were in a small entrance, she could see through to a bedroom. The large room was dominated by a massive bed, rumpled now by the prince's fitful sleep. The air was redolent with the scent of warm, somnolent male.

She crossed her arms, suddenly a little too aware of her state of undress and of the partially clad man standing too close for comfort. Her eyes flicked up to his and she saw him swallow. A glimmer of awareness danced between them, as unwelcome as a skunk in church.

Her breath became shallow and quick, nerves she hoped, and not attraction.

But oh, Prince Aleksandre was most definitely attractive. The cover models on her romance novels couldn't begin to compare to this man. She didn't want to stare, but she couldn't help it. He was a beautiful male specimen. Her gaze roamed over his honed shoulders and chest and down to the hard ridges of his belly. What she saw there made her gasp.

"Aleks!" Without a thought to the impropriety, she touched the thick, ragged mass of scars along the left side of his belly. "You've been hurt. Badly."

In a steel grip, his hand trapped hers against his hot skin. "It's nothing."

"Don't lie." She looked up at his hard face. No wonder he'd changed. "What happened? Tell me."

His nostrils flared.

"War is ugly, even for those who lead. My men and I were hit by a grenade." Briefly, his eyes squeezed shut as if the memory was too much to bear.

She studied his face, wondering what other secrets lay behind the aloof facade of Prince Aleksandre. He had suffered, too. He'd been hurt, badly wounded in war. A war that had occurred while she was pregnant with Nico. The ramifications of that were something she needed to think about.

A powerful desire to kneel at his side and kiss the wounds set her to trembling.

"I should go." But her fingers were trapped beneath his, and the feel of his hot flesh was a powerful aphrodisiac.

"No." His lips barely moved but his eyes glittered like onyx in sunlight.

She had to get out of here before she did something totally inappropriate. She tugged. He held on.

"Am I under house arrest or something?"

A short laugh escaped him, dispelling some of the tension.

He lifted her hand from his side but didn't release it. "You wouldn't make it back to your room right now. Sit down. You've overdone. You're shaking."

She most certainly was. "My side hurts a little."

The incision was as good an excuse as any.

He motioned to a chair and guided her down. The heat from his hand burned into her skin long after he stepped away.

"You shouldn't have come up here."

He was right about that.

"I need to see my son."

A hint of a smile lifted his mouth. "You are a single-minded woman."

She'd thought so, too, but five minutes with Aleks had her brain scrambled. Here, alone in his apartments, without the trappings of royalty around him, he was so much more approachable, more human, and much more the Aleks she'd loved.

"I will never do anything to hurt Nico. Let me see him at will. Whether you believe me or not, I love him. I would willingly give him my heart if that's what he needed."

"For compensation."

"Let's not have this argument again. I do not want your blood money." She touched her side. "My intentions should be clear by now."

And if he hadn't figured out that those intentions were good, there was nothing she could do about it.

He said nothing for several beats of time, but his glittering eyes watched her like a cat deciding if a mouse was worthy of his attention. She could see the wheels turning, thinking of the payment he'd promised, as though that mattered to her.

"Is this invasion of my bedroom a ploy to upset me or are you truly concerned for Nico? My mother suspects you have ulterior motives—beyond the payment, of course."

"She doesn't like me."

One eyebrow rose imperiously. "For good reason."

Sara bent forward in the chair, cradling her side, though perversely glad for the aching reminder that she had finally done something right for her child. "I made a terrible mistake."

"Indeed."

"Regardless of what you believe, Aleks, I didn't think you were coming back. I never received any messages from you. Nothing. I lost hope." And now she wondered, had the warrior prince been too ill to contact her? But if so, how had he gained custody of Nico?

Again, that pensive silence and then in a faraway murmur, he said, "I wish I could believe that."

So did she.

"You said our relationship was nothing but a fling."

He went still, his gaze somewhere in the distance. When he spoke, the word was soft and held no rancor, but it cut just the same. "True."

Regardless of his fury at her for putting Nico up for adoption, the prince himself had never intended to return.

"I'll go." She stood and headed for the door. Aleks remained where he was.

As she started out, she heard him sigh.

"Go to Nico," he said. "I'll be there as soon I've dressed."

# CHAPTER FIVE

"SHE WAS SEEN COMING from your rooms, Aleksandre. What are you thinking? You've fallen under her spell again, haven't you?"

"Don't be foolish."

Last night had rattled him, but his mother was already distressed enough. He would certainly not tell her as much. Sara in her white gown and flowing red hair had stirred his desire as well as his memory. When she'd touched his scars and looked at him with wide, compassionate eyes, he'd been sorely tempted to pull her into his arms and tell her every place inside him that hurt.

Thank heaven, he hadn't. Her nearness was like a drug that addled his senses. In the light of day, he could better recall the myriad reasons for remaining impersonal with the lovely Miss Presley.

But more than this, he'd been rattled by her dogged devotion to Nico. Within hours after surgery, she'd insisted on sitting at his bedside, one hand touching his limp fingers, her eyes brimming with tears.

He didn't understand this. He didn't understand her. Why would a woman discard a baby and four years later behave this way? Guilt?

Once she'd breached Nico's sickroom last night, she'd refused to leave until dawn. The boy was restless, she'd said, and needed her. He suspected Maria was partly the reason for her determined stay. Sara didn't trust Carlo's mother, an ungrounded reaction, and more proof of how misguided he'd been to fall for the American in the first place. She was the untrustworthy one, not Maria.

Maria was the most loyal person in his castle. Like mother, like son. Because of Carlo's heroic sacrifice, the Prince of Carvainia would care for Maria all the days of her life.

The memory of Carlo, his best friend and bodyguard, brought both pain and gladness and dreadful guilt. No friend could ever be as faithful as the man who'd laid down his life for his monarch.

"Aleksandre, please." His mother, his greatest ally, was unstoppable when she'd set her mind to something. Such had been the case when she'd rescued Nico from America. Such was also the case with the reappearance of Nico's birth mother. Though grateful to see her grandson beginning to recover, the topic of Sara turned her into a nag. "What was Sara Presley doing in your room?"

"We were making passionate love."

The queen sucked in a shocked gasp. "Aleksandre!"

He bowed slightly. "I'm sorry, Mother. That was uncalled for and untrue."

And he desperately wished he hadn't put the image in his mind. He was having quite enough trouble with Sara Presley as it was.

Thanks to her, he was exhausted, though not from lovemaking. He might be in a less cranky mood had it been thus. Other than carrying Sara out of Nico's room kicking and screaming, there was little he could do last night but doze in a chair and wait for morning. When he had awakened at sunup from an erotic dream to find Sara still in nightgown and bare feet, it had been all he could do to escape the room with his dignity.

Suddenly, the door to his office burst open without the usual protocol. The prince whirled, on guard and ready for attack.

A harried-looking attendant cried, "Your Majesty, you must come. Nico has taken a turn for the worse."

Late the next evening, Sara's eyes felt like sandpaper and she thought she might fall out of the chair positioned next to Nico's bedside. The little prince had finally rallied after a sudden, unexpected bout of vomiting. The doctors were bewildered but vials of blood were drawn to be certain the new liver was still functioning.

Sara folded her hands in silent prayer. *Please, please, please, let him be all right.*

An hour ago, the haughty Queen Irena had finally departed, though her dark eyes shot daggers at Sara as she swept out of the room.

Aleks himself sat, arms folded, long legs extended, as tired as she, though he would die before he'd admit it.

"You should go to bed, Sara. You're still recovering, too."

"Since when did you start caring?" She bit the words out, tired, achy and a little depressed. The past week had been harder than she'd imagined.

To her surprise, his tired eyes twinkled as he said, "Can't have an American die on foreign soil. You could create an international incident."

Her answer was a droll, "Now you tell me."

He chuckled. The sound lifted her flagging spirits. Was the ice man finally thawing or was he too exhausted to sustain his fury against her? "The nurse will remain with Nico. Dr.

Konstantine thinks the crisis is over and he will sleep the night. You must leave now."

"You're tired, too. I'll go if you'll go."

One aristocratic eyebrow lifted. "Since when did you start caring?"

Was he teasing her? The man must be delirious.

She wanted to tell him the truth—that she'd never stopped caring—but she feared the admission would drive him back into that shell.

"Can't have a ruling prince die on me. It might cause a national uprising."

His mouth curved. He rose and held out a hand. "Come. I'll see you to your suite."

An uneasy truce developed with Aleks, but Sara had no illusions that he trusted her, or even that she was welcome in Carvainia. Most of her visits with Nico were supervised by Queen Irena, a watchful, suspicious woman who had only spoken to Sara once, and that was to ask when she was leaving.

This was a worry that plagued Sara as she recovered from her surgery. After three weeks, she felt completely well, but if she said as much, would she be expected to leave? The thought unhinged her. Now that she was here, she never wanted to return to America. Her heart was in Carvainia.

By the third week post-op, the little prince was up and around, having recoverd from two bouts of mysterious vomiting that the doctors could not attribute to the surgery or to the antirejection drugs. Each day the boy's complexion gained more healthy color and, according to Antonia, the nation buzzed with the good news that their beloved prince would recover.

This particular day, Sara and Nico had ventured onto the

balcony to sit in the sunshine and listen to the sea. She'd brought along a deck of cards and was teaching Nico to play Go Fish. Aleks stood at the balcony railing watching the seabirds dip and call along the sandy shore.

"Papa, do come and play. Sara knows the funnest games."

Aleks turned, his expression unreadable as he corrected the grammar. "Most fun games."

The little prince nodded. "Will you play with us?"

"Your grandmother will be here soon. I have a meeting with the parliament in a while."

Though a royal, Prince Aleksandre was not a man of leisure. His duties often kept him away or up late at night, but he spent every extra moment with Nico. Today, he looked particularly tired. His son's illness had taken a tremendous toll on him.

"One game, Papa, just one. Please."

Aleks pulled out a chair from the round patio table and joined them. "Deal me in."

Sara shot him an amused glance as she counted out five cards for each person. "A poker-playing prince?"

"Only when the stakes are high." He didn't offer a smile, and Sara had a feeling he was talking about her, about taking the risk of bringing her to Carvainia.

"Some risks are worth everything." She pointedly slid her gaze to the recovering child.

With a tilt of his head, Aleks lifted his cards. "Indeed."

Oblivious to the byplay between the adults, Nico said, "May I go first, Miss Sara?"

"Yes, you may."

"Do you have any fours? I'm four." He held up four splayed fingers. "My birthday was March tenth. I was sick."

The reminder sent a spear through Sara's heart. She'd

missed every birthday but one. "I'm so glad you're better now. The next birthday will be a grand celebration, I'm sure."

She handed over a pair of the requested card and watched like a proud mother as Nico triumphantly counted out a complete set.

"One, two, free, *four*." He put the last card down with emphasis and grinned. "I'm going to win. Papa says a warrior prince must always win. When I'm big I shall be a warrior prince, won't I, Papa?"

Sara shivered at the thought of her son at war. "Let's hope for peace instead." She quickly reverted to the game, asking Aleks, "Do you have any queens?"

"None at the moment," Aleks replied. "Though I am searching. Go Fish."

Nico giggled with glee and high-fived his father, the very small hand colliding against the large, strong one in a resounding smack.

With a short laugh, Sara drew a card from the pile in the center and added it to her hand. "Are the royals ganging up on the poor commoner?"

This time Aleks laughed, too.

"Beware of the guillotine. We royals can be ruthless."

He confused her, this prince of Carvainia. One minute he was as cold as Antarctica and then for a brief, unguarded moment, he'd become the man she'd known and loved in college.

At the end of the game, he glanced at his watch. "I must go, son. Perhaps we can play again tomorrow."

"Sara said tomorrow we could walk along the seashore and gather shells."

"Oh, she did, did she?"

"With your permission, of course," Sara hurried to add. "Little boys get tired of being indoors."

"And what would you know of little boys?" he asked quietly.

Sara blanched at the intentional jab but she stared him down. "Not nearly as much as I'd like to. Thanks to you."

His gaze hardened. "You have only yourself to blame."

Suddenly, Nico clapped his little hands together. "Let's make a picnic and go in the boat."

Aleks stiffened. "I don't think that's a good idea."

"Sara won't capsize the boat this time, will you, Sara?" Big dark eyes beseeched her.

Sara gulped, unsure of how to answer. From Aleks's black expression he was no more enamored of the idea than she. Being with him in the sickroom was one thing, but an afternoon of fun with Aleks could open up a Pandora's box of emotions. In her current state, she wasn't sure she could handle them. Every glimpse of the real Aleks pulled at her like a powerful magnet. Even this new and princely Aleks had moments when she feared that she could love him, too.

And for a plain bookstore owner to love a prince could only bring more heartache.

"Will you, Sara? Say you won't capsize the boat, so Papa will agree. Please."

The child's pleading pulled at her. Poor little man. He thought his father was reluctant because of the long-ago overturned boat. He had no idea that the incident had been one of her best memories, the prelude to a weekend of love she would never forget…or regret.

She treasured her memories of Aleks, but how much longer would she have to make memories with this sweet son of hers?

If Aleks's behavior was any indication, not nearly long enough.

"I would do my best not to cause a problem," she said.

"See, Papa, see? Please say yes. We will have a jolly good time."

Sara could see the war raging inside the prince. He wanted to please his son, but he did not want to be with her. Nor did she want to be with him, though she suspected their reasons for avoidance differed greatly.

Relenting, she said, "I'm not a good sailor, Nico." A lie. "Perhaps you and your father should take the picnic alone."

"No!" The little prince was growing agitated. "I want you."

Those simple words meant more than the child could ever know. He was growing attached to her. She was both glad and afraid. How would he react when Aleks decided her time in Carvainia was over and she had to leave? Worse, what would he think of her someday in the future when he discovered the name of his birth mother, because as sure as his father had the power to adopt him, the son would have the power to ferret out the truth of his birth.

"I want Sara, Papa. And you and me."

Aleksandre's mouth flattened into a tight line. He glared at Sara as he placed a hand on Nico's shoulder. "Do not upset yourself. I'll see what I can arrange."

With that, he spun on his heel and left.

Bright and early the next morning as the first members of the castle staff began to stir, Sara slipped from her bed to shower and dress. While she showered, someone—Antonia, no doubt—had delivered a silver coffee carafe, pastry and fruit. Hair still damp, Sara poured a cup of the fragrant French brew and stepped out on the balcony.

Greeted by the sound of the rushing sea and the pale pinks and grays of dawn, she sipped at her coffee and breathed in the peaceful morning. Last night, she'd talked to Penny by telephone for over an hour. Her friend thought she was crazy to remain in Carvainia in the company of powerful people who clearly despised her. And yet, Penny had also understood. The son she'd mourned for was here.

"What about Aleks?" Penny had asked.

"What about him?"

"Do you still feel—you know—attracted to him?"

"I'd be lying if I said no."

"Oh, girl. I feel so bad that I talked you into this trip."

"I'm glad you did."

"You're going to get hurt."

"Nothing could hurt more than four years of not knowing where my son was."

But this morning, Sara realized the statement hadn't been true. Losing him a second time was going to be worse. Before, she hadn't known him. This time, she did. She knew what made him giggle in that cute little boy way, with his head tilted back and his eyes scrunched shut. She knew how bright he was and his favorite color and the sound of voice and the smell of his hair. She knew too much.

In another ten minutes, the sun would pop over the horizon. Down below, along the water's edge, she spotted a tall, shadowy form. Aleks. Back turned, facing out to sea, he stood with his hands in his pockets, a forlorn figure. He looked as though he carried the weight of the world—and in a way he did. At least the world as Carvainians knew it. He had great power, but with that power came great responsibility. She'd never thought of that before.

Aleks would take responsibility very seriously.

She set her coffee cup aside and watched him for a long time, her heart calling out to him. Though tempted to slip out into the soft morning and stand beside him, she refrained. She could do nothing for the father. But the son was a different matter.

Five minutes later, she reached the medical floor. The dim

morning light battled with the pale night lamps illuminating the corridors. No security was posted at Nico's door, a concession to his recovery and the time of day, she supposed, though definitely a change of protocol.

The elevator slid quietly closed behind her. As she started toward Nico's room, a woman appeared from the staircase on the left. Something in her hurried, furtive movements gave Sara pause. She stepped back into the shadows.

Curious, Sara watched the woman glance around before quickly entering Nico's room. In the dim light, Sara could not make out the woman's face, but she was tall and moved with an almost haughty grace. Queen Irena? The nurse, Maria? She was tall, but so were many of the Carvainian women Sara had met. The secretive woman could be anyone.

The question was, why the secretive behavior?

Unease prickled Sara's skin. She hurried down the corridor and pushed open Nico's door.

Except for the sleeping child, the room was empty.

# CHAPTER SIX

ALEKS WAS BEWILDERED by his own behavior. He should never have agreed to a boating picnic with Sara Presley along. Yet here he was, rowing lazily around the small, private cove a short distance from the castle proper while Sara listened to Nico's enthusiastic chatter and tried to keep him still inside the boat.

Seeing Nico with this much energy thrilled him. The improved health also assuaged some of his guilt. Had he not taken Nico into the flood-ravaged areas of Carvainia last year, the boy would not have contracted the virus that destroyed his liver. In trying to teach his son compassion for those in need and the duty of a prince to care for his people, he'd nearly cost Nico his life. He wasn't sure he could ever forgive himself for that crucial error in judgment, but he would be eternally grateful that his son had been spared.

His gaze went to Sara. He could thank *her* for that.

She looked up just then and smiled. Something stirred inside him and without thinking, he smiled back.

"I've seen this cove from my balcony," she said, brushing back tiny wisps of dusky red hair from her temples. "It's really beautiful here."

Yes, he'd seen her standing on the railed balcony each morning, usually in that flowing white gown that haunted him. Today, long before dawn, she'd been dressed and drinking coffee. According to Antonia, an able spy when need be, Sara hadn't changed that much since he'd known her. She still preferred coffee to tea and a hamburger to the finest steak.

He wondered if she still mumbled in her sleep.

"I always thought you would like it here." The words appeared on their own, shaking him.

At her quizzical look he gave himself to the oars and pushed his arm muscles as hard as possible, hoping the burn would take control and keep him from saying anything else he might regret. His mother was more correct than she realized. Sara Presley was getting to him.

"Papa, if I stand up, will the boat tip over?"

"Possibly. Stay seated. We'll dock in that small nook just there." He hitched his chin toward a tiny clearing shrouded in brush and trees. The area was invisible from the castle and security would not be pleased with his breach, though they should know by now he could take care of himself.

Sara slipped an arm around Nico's shoulder and snugged him close to her side. "Let's sing a song. Do you know 'Row, Row, Row Your Boat'?"

Nico looked doubtful. "No."

"What?" She flicked a look of mock horror toward Aleks. "You've neglected this boy's education."

Aleks's lips twitched. "Fire the tutor."

"No, Papa! I like Mr. Benois."

Sara laughed, a light, easy sound that he remembered too well. "Your father is teasing, Nico. Come on, now. I will sing a line and you repeat after me."

In a sweet, clear soprano, she began to sing the familiar

song, pausing while Nico echoed each phrase in a childish, happy voice.

As he guided the boat onto land, Aleks heard his own baritone join in. Both Nico and Sara looked up in pleased surprise.

In that moment, he saw what he'd never seen before, what he'd never wanted to see.

A mother and son. And the son had Sara's radiant, full-mouthed smile.

His belly sank like the anchor he'd tossed overboard.

"Papa is singing. Papa is singing." Nico clapped his hands. Sara laughed.

And Prince Aleksandre sang a little louder just to watch them smile again.

Sara had stewed all morning about the mysterious woman who had entered Nico's room and disappeared. The incident made no sense, and in the light of day, she questioned whether she'd seen anything at all.

"What did the chef pack for us?" Aleks asked, as he spread a blue blanket on the soft, flower-specked grass. A gold family crest centered the cloth.

"I didn't look in the basket, but I'm sure it's wonderful," she said. "Everything here is."

"Everything?"

"Well, practically."

His answer was a twitched eyebrow and a few crinkles at the corners of his eyes.

He was different today. She couldn't quite put her finger on the change. He hadn't wanted this outing and yet he seemed to be enjoying himself…as was she, though her uncertain future nagged at the back of her brain like an itch she couldn't scratch.

According to the physicians, she should rest and recover under their care for two months. Half of that was nearly gone.

A shudder stole through her. One more month before the doctors released her—and then what? Would Aleks agree to let her remain a part of Nico's life? Or would she be forced back to the lonely life in a bookstore, forever without her son?

The longer she was here, the harder leaving would be. And Nico wasn't the only reason. As confused and hurt and angry as Aleks could make her, her heart remembered a time of love.

Occasionally she caught glimpses of just plain, wonderful, loving Aleks beneath the princely facade, and hope would rise inside her as powerful as a volcano and just as dangerous. She couldn't trust herself with this man who'd left her alone without a word at a crucial time. Even if he'd been to war, even if he'd been wounded, he was still a powerful man. If he had intended to return as he claimed, if he had truly cared for her, couldn't he have sent word?

Sara sighed and opened the lid on the picnic basket. What was the point in rehashing the unchangeable past?

He was a prince. She was no one. Men of his position only played with commoners. They did not marry them.

The truth was as painful as a burn in her chest. Aleks had wanted her body for a while, and that was all. He'd never expected a child to come from their loving.

An insect buzzed her ear. She swatted at it, swatting away the sorrowful thoughts as she kept a watchful eye on Nico. As any small boy would, the little prince wandered around the pretty little meadow, poking at rocks and gathering flowers and weeds into a tight fist. Though he was still far too thin and tired easily, her heart jumped with happiness to see him doing well.

She stretched her arms above her head, feeling only the

slight tug of scar tissue at her side, and breathed in the fragrance of sea salt and lush, green meadow. A floral scent she didn't recognize tickled her nose.

"What is that flower I smell?" she asked.

Aleks eased down onto the blanket and stretched his long legs before him. Sara battled a flash of memory. The two of them, a blanket by a lake, the hot summer night pulsing with the beat of two hearts and a hundred whispered promises.

Promises that had been broken.

Aleks sniffed the air. "Delicate and sweet with a hint of fruit?"

"You sound like a perfumer."

He chuckled. "Wine connoisseur. The scent comes from the vineyards. Muscato grapes for spumante."

Another reminder of why she didn't fit in his world. She wouldn't know a spumante from a bottle of beer.

"It smells great," she said, and then felt stupid for the mundane comment.

She bit down on her bottom lip and began to unpack the basket, setting out a stunning array of silver and china and scrumptious foodstuffs. Royalty never skimped. Even something as simple as a picnic was a major production.

The prince said nothing, but he watched her from beneath those enviable black lashes with a pensive expression.

Wondering what went on behind those dark eyes and uncomfortable with the silent stare, Sara threw a napkin at him—a crested cloth napkin in royal blue. "Make yourself useful, Mr. Prince."

The expression disappeared. He shifted closer. "You always were a demanding woman."

His easy reference to their past caught her off guard. "Was I?"

"No." He pulled a bottle of wine from the basket and studied the label. "Quite the contrary. Perhaps if you had been…"

Sara's heart clattered in her chest like a marble in a tin can. What was he saying? That if she'd demanded more, she would have got it?

But that wasn't her way. She believed love was a gift. If he had loved her enough, he would have gone on loving her, regardless of time and distance, the way she had gone on loving him.

The thought brought her up short. Was she still in love with Aleksandre d'Gabriel?

Her gaze flicked to his and then away to stare at an iridescent dragonfly flitting along the shore.

By all that was good, she hoped not. Her greatest fear was to become vulnerable to him again. He'd hurt her before, but this time, with Nico involved, he could destroy her. He was arrogant and curt and loathed her. How could she even consider loving a man such as that?

A little voice whispered inside her heart. She could love him because she'd known the man beneath the prince. And he was wonderful and brave and good. No other man had ever made her feel as precious and loved. He *had* loved her then, perhaps not in the way she'd thought, perhaps far more selfishly, but he had loved her.

And her traitorous heart could not forget.

"Papa, come quick." Nico's excited voice interrupted. "I found something."

Sara's hand went to her chest. "I hope it's not a snake."

With a half laugh, Aleks pushed to his feet. "We have no snakes in Carvainia. They were banished by proclamation."

She looked up the tall length of him. "Is that true?"

Eyes dancing in a way that filled her with foolish, foolish yearning, he reached out a hand. "Come and see for yourself."

She put her hand in his and he pulled her up. She expected him to release his hold, but he tugged her across the sweet-scented grass toward their son.

Her heart skittered in her chest. *Their* son. She couldn't help wondering what life would have been like if Aleks had never left America, if they had married, if the three of them were a family.

But they weren't. And regardless of her silly fantasies, Aleks was no longer the man she recalled any more than she was the same, gullible college girl. By Aleks's own admission, he had played her for a fool even then—a rich, international playboy having his fling with a naive American. He'd no more expected the liaison to result in a child than she had.

He had known what she hadn't. He was a royal, no doubt expected to marry royal. American college girls were only playmates.

An ache much greater than the pain of surgery stole her breath.

She tugged her hand from Aleks's grip. He gave her a puzzled look, but they had reached Nico and his attention went to the little boy. Squatted beside a mound of rocks and weeds, hands on his thighs, Nico peered intently at the ground.

"What have you found, son?" Aleks asked, going to his haunches, too.

"That." Without turning his head, Nico pointed a finger. "Will it bite me?"

Above the two dark heads, Sara bent low enough to see a small turtle. Aleks reached into the grass and picked it up. The animal promptly withdrew into its shell.

Nico gasped and turned huge black eyes on his father. "Papa, what did you do to him?"

From her vantage point, Sara could see the side of Aleks's face. His cheeks creased in an indulgent smile.

"We frightened him." Holding the turtle with a thumb and middle finger, he offered the animal to Nico. "He won't bite unless you put your finger in his mouth."

In total awe, Nico took the two-inch reptile in both his small hands. He lifted the shell to eye level and peeked inside. "Come out. I'm not a mean boy."

Sara's chest squeezed at the sweetness. How many of these moments had she missed? "Is this your first time to find a turtle?"

He nodded, but his focus remained on his father. "May I keep him?"

Aleks shook his head. "No. He would not be happy living in the castle."

Nico seemed taken aback. "But we have the finest castle in the world."

"A turtle is a wild animal. His castle, his home is here in the weeds and rocks."

Nico's face grew long and somber. "But I would be kind to him."

To soften the refusal, Aleks placed a wide hand on the back of his son's neck. With infinite patience he said, "Would you be happy if someone took you away from your home and family? Even if it was a nice place with kind people?"

Sara listened with a terrible intensity. Though afraid she could never gain custody of her child, hadn't she considered attempting exactly that?

The little boy thought it over and then placed the turtle on the ground. "I would be sad to ever, ever leave you, Papa."

And though the mother-wound in her heart bled, that was the moment Sara knew that she could never take Nico away from Carvainia, even if such a thing was possible. He belonged here, with his father and his people.

"My son, you have a strong and kind heart." Aleks

tenderly pulled Nico into his arms. "You will make a wise ruler someday."

*Like father, like son.* The way it should be. And she, though mother by Nico's birth, was an outsider.

The realization nearly brought her to her knees. Just as Aleks had indicated early on, she was nothing but a hired body part.

A short time later, the three of them, along with Nico's turtle as temporary guest, gathered around the picnic basket. Sara bit into an elegant smoked salmon sandwich with cream cheese and nearly moaned from the experience. Though her heart was heavy, her stomach seemed determined to make the most of her dream "vacation."

"Nico," she said, holding out another. "You should try this. It's quite delicious."

He'd hardly eaten anything.

Nico shook his head as he placed one hand to his belly. "My stomach feels strange."

Salmon forgotten in an instant, Sara was up on her knees with a hand to Nico's forehead. She exchanged concerned glances with Aleks. "No fever."

"Are you tired?" Aleks asked, laying aside his own sandwich. "Perhaps we should go back to the castle now."

"I don't want to go yet. I like it here." Nico's bottom lip poked out in an uncharacteristic pout. "I'm not hungry."

Sara longed to take the boy onto her lap and soothe him, but before she could, Aleks said, "Then why don't you play quietly with Mr. Turtle while Sara and I finish our meal. If your stomach bothers you further, you must tell us right away."

Nico looked doubtful. "I don't want Dr. Konstantine to come. I don't like needle sticks."

What could anyone say to that? The child had been through enough to last two lifetimes.

Aleks retrieved his sandwich, though guilt and helplessness pinched his face.

Turtle clutched to his chest, Nico wandered slowly toward the shoreline.

Sara followed him with a worried gaze. "He's not usually fussy like that."

"No. His behavior concerns me."

"I'm concerned, too, Aleks, but for other reasons." She picked at a crust of bread. He needed to hear her suspicions even if he thought she was crazy. "I need to ask you something. Or rather, tell you something."

He sat up straighter, immediately on guard. "About Nico?"

"About these strange bouts of illness that the doctors can't explain."

"They are a puzzle—and a worry."

She popped a tiny piece of bread into her mouth, chewed and swallowed, unsure of how to approach the subject. Would Aleks think she was trying to cause a problem? Would he believe her?

Neither mattered. If there was the remotest possibility that Nico was in danger, she had to tell Aleks.

Swallowing her tension, she asked, "Have you ever considered that someone might want to harm Nico?"

The air around the warrior prince stilled. Eyes narrowed in suspicion, he leaned toward her. "What are you talking about?"

So fierce was his stare that she trembled. Any threat to the royal heir would not be taken lightly and she could almost feel sorry for anyone who crossed the prince of Carvainia.

When she hesitated, his jaw flexed. "Speak, woman!"

Sara's tongue flicked out over lips gone dry as the Sahara.

"All right, but you may not like what I have to say. Twice before when Nico's stomach hurt, he had been tended by Maria during the preceding hours. And then this morning I saw someone go into his room. I thought the person might have been her."

Skepticism replaced some of his intensity. "There is nothing sinister in that. Maria is devoted to the little prince just as her son was devoted to me."

"But Nico was sick after her visits. Twice."

"A coincidence. Nothing more. In case you've forgotten, he's been a very sick boy. Maria is devoted to him and has nursed him tirelessly since this nightmare began."

"But what if her devotion is a ploy to do him harm?"

Aleks slammed a fist into his palm. "Enough! You have no idea what you're saying."

Pulse clattering and more than a little nervous at rousing his ire, Sara refused to back down. He might be the all-powerful Oz but he did not rule her. "Then enlighten me. What's so special about this woman?"

"Her son."

"And who might that be?"

His jaw clenched and unclenched, as though he held back great emotion. "Carlo. You remember."

"Carlo? Your friend? Of course, I do." The image of a stocky young man with a wrestler's build formed in her head. "He was very quiet, but a nice guy. A gentle giant."

The prince's voice dropped to a murmur. "The best friend I ever had."

The past tense was not lost on Sara. Dread pulled at her gut. "What happened to him?"

"He died saving my life."

His tortured expression shattered Sara's restraint. She knew how close he and Carlo had been. She also knew Aleks would feel responsible for his friend's death, whether he was or not.

With no thought of the wall that now separated them, Sara moved to his side, circling him with her arms, her need to comfort overriding the fear of rejection.

When Aleks didn't resist, she laid her head on his shoulder and whispered, "I am terribly sorry."

One of his strong, warrior's hands came up to press her back, bringing her closer.

"As am I."

The admission was barely a whisper against her hair, the tension in his body rock hard and thrumming with leashed emotion.

She closed her eyes against the unexpected wash of feelings. No matter the years and sorrows between them, she still loved the scent and texture of his skin, the corded strength of him, the depth of character that had made her love him with every fiber of her being.

She touched his side, remembering the knotty, horrid scars. Aleks flinched but didn't pull away. Instead he buried his face in her hair and sighed, his breath warm against her scalp.

"The grenade that hurt you," she murmured. "Was that when it happened?"

Beneath the smooth cloth of his shirt, the scars were easily felt along the honed ridges of his ribs and belly. With a light touch, her fingers studied the shape and breadth of his terrible wounds, massaging gently as if to erase his pain and memories.

"Yes. Then." She heard him swallow. "Carlo threw himself on the grenade to protect me. I was injured but he was killed. He died in service to his ruler, but more than that, he gave his life for a friend."

He lifted his head and Sara saw the suffering caused by

Carlo's sacrifice. She saw something else, too, and her pulse quickened as Aleks's pupils dilated and his gaze flicked to her mouth.

Could he possibly want to kiss her? Did she want him to?

It was her turn to swallow. Her lips parted. Then, as if her acceptance was a turnoff, Aleks gently but firmly pulled away.

The sense of loss stunned her. In that brief moment in Aleks's arms, she'd longed, not only for his kiss, but for his love.

Wouldn't she ever learn? She turned to the side and pressed a fist against her trembling mouth.

After a few seconds of loud silence, Aleks cleared his throat.

"So," he said, as though nothing personal had transpired, as though he'd felt nothing in those sweet moments. Perhaps he hadn't. "You can understand why I trust Maria with my son's life."

She did understand. And yet the strong feeling that something was amiss would not go away.

Reining in her emotions, Sara turned back toward the prince. If he was unaffected, so was she. Nico was the important one here, not them.

"Could there be anyone else who might want to harm Nico?"

"The little prince, as the people call him, is the darling of Carvainia. You've seen the papers and the television. You've seen the thousands of cards and gifts that have poured in from all over the country."

Sara sighed and pushed at her hair, frustrated. He was right. Who would want to harm an adorable four-year-old boy?

She gave a small, uncertain laugh. "Maybe I've become an overprotective mother, seeing danger around every corner."

Aleks cut a sharp glance toward Nico, who was out of hearing range. "The only person with power to hurt Nico is you. Kindly mind what you say in his presence."

His reaction both hurt and angered. "He didn't hear me."

"And you should be glad he didn't."

The callous remark incensed her. "Exactly what would you do if he *did* hear me? If he found out the truth?"

Fury flushed his dark skin. "Do not challenge me, Sara Presley. This is not a game you can win."

Face burning and tears pushing at the back of her eyelids, Sara dropped her head and began shoving picnic items into the basket. She didn't want him to know how upset she was, not only because he refused to see how much she cared for Nico, but because they were fighting again, their truce broken. She'd thought they were moving toward... friendship, but she'd been wrong. Aleks would always despise her.

"Papa." Nico came toward them, one hand on his abdomen. His skin had turned the color of ashes. He stopped and bent over.

Sara jumped to her feet and hurried to him. "What's wrong? Are you sick? Do you hurt?"

Aleks was beside her in a flash, arriving just as the child pitched forward into Sara's arms and began to retch.

After an infusion prescribed by Dr. Konstantine and a call to the liver specialist, the mysterious illness disappeared almost as quickly as it had come.

Aleks was beside himself with worry as he stalked back and forth in his office, contemplating the day's events.

Sara Presley's bizarre suspicions had unnerved him. That could be the only explanation for his irrational behavior.

He leaned both hands against his desk and stared down at the gleaming surface. Sara's pale and lovely face seemed to stare back.

He gritted his teeth. What was she doing to him?

In that brief interval in her arms, he'd felt whole again, the raging guilt and anger and sorrow soothed by her touch.

He slammed a hand against the desktop, the sound echoing in the room as he fought back the raw emotions that only Sara Presley had ever stirred in him.

She was a liar, a traitor, a woman who'd abandoned his son. He could not allow himself to be seduced by her sweetness. A principality and a crown were at stake, as well as his heart and his son.

She was wrong about Maria, wrong about everything. She had to be. No one would wish harm upon a four-year-old child.

A terrible voice whispered inside his head. *Unless that child was the son of an old and still-hated enemy.*

"I want a list of everyone who has been in Nico's rooms," he said, barking out the command.

"Your Majesty?" His secretary, Jonas La Blanc, stood at attention beside a computer desk—his work space when the prince was doing correspondence. His bland face showed no reaction to his leader's obvious disturbance.

"I want to know who is in Nico's rooms and when. I want a full report for as far back as you can get it and from this moment forward. And I do not want you to explain this to anyone. Simply do it."

"As you wish, sir." The man bowed and backed away several steps before turning to leave the room.

La Blanc probably thought him mad. Maybe he was. Sara Presley was driving him insane.

Aleks waited until the door soughed shut and then squeezed the bridge of his nose.

She had rattled him, and now his mind jumped from the feel of her in his arms to her dogged insistence that someone might want to harm Nico. Surely no one on his staff, no one in this household would be so diabolical. And yet, Carvainia had enemies. *He* had enemies.

Though they had enjoyed several years of peace, the king of Perseidia had signed their treaty under duress. He was by no means a friend. Had a spy infiltrated the castle?

He shuddered. What if even now an assassin plotted evil against the crown prince.

"No!" He slammed his fist against the stone fireplace. Sara Presley had put paranoid thoughts into his mind. She was the enemy within the walls, seeking to disrupt his household and create dissension.

*But she cares for Nico.*

The thought hit him like a cannonball. Though he'd fought against believing anything good about her, he could not deny her devotion to the boy—unless that devotion came with an ulterior motive.

He rubbed the tight, tight muscles in his neck.

Were Sara's actions truthful? Were her suspicions spoken because she cared for Nico, or because she sought revenge on the father for perceived wrongs?

At this moment, he didn't know what to believe.

He'd watched Sara at Nico's bedside, still recovering from her own surgery and yet determined to nurse the sick boy. He'd heard her crooning soft words and tender songs when Nico cried with pain. And then today, when Nico had fallen ill, it was Sara who'd held him on her lap while Aleks rowed them back to the castle. It was Sara Nico had reached for.

His gut clenched. Nico wasn't the only one who wanted Sara. He, the leader of a nation, a man in control, could not seem to control his thoughts and emotions when it came to one particular American woman.

But experience didn't lie. She had been false before.

With a groan of frustration, he stormed out of his office and headed toward the security center. He couldn't decide the best course of action with Sara, but he was taking no chances with his son.

## CHAPTER SEVEN

SARA HELD NICO'S HAND as they strolled through the vineyards on their way to the children's garden. In the days since Nico's last bout of illness, his color had improved, his energy increased, and he'd become restless in the sickroom.

A boy needed to be outdoors in the sunshine and fresh air. A boy needed to run and play. She was happy to give him those opportunities.

Nico was not quite as lively as she'd have liked, but he kicked at dirt clods and paused frequently to investigate a bug or a plant or anthill. He was curious about everything, brilliant child that he was.

"What is that bird, Miss Sara?" he asked, head back, shading his eyes with one small hand.

"I'm not sure." She turned to the male nurse who trailed them. "Do you know, Mr. Chang?"

The man, who looked strong enough to hoist a car, glanced upward. "A swift, I believe."

"There you have it, Nico. A swift."

"What about that one?" He pointed to another.

"That one I know. A blue jay."

"And that one?"

She laughed. "I'm afraid I don't know. You must ask your father for a bird book."

"Papa had a meeting with Count Regis."

"Yes. But you'll see him today. He always has time for his favorite son." It was one of the things she admired about Aleks—one of too many. Though the demands on his time were heavy, he popped in to see Nico often throughout the day. He was a good father. All the years of worrying about her baby's welfare had been wasted.

Nico giggled, one sweet hand to his lips in that charming manner of his. "I'm his *only* son, Miss Sara."

She pretended surprise. "Well, my goodness, I guess you are."

She'd been surprised to say the least when Aleks had telephoned her room this morning with the news that his presence was no longer required for her to visit Nico. Did this mean he trusted her? Or that he could no longer stand the sight of her?

Since the picnic, he'd kept his distance, saying little when they were together, but she could practically feel the wheels turning inside his head.

"Look, Miss Sara, the garden." Nico pulled away then and rushed off, short legs churning the grass.

Mr. Chang sprinted quickly after him, remaining watchfully by his side. Sara suspected Chang was more bodyguard than nurse, though she was not privy to such information.

When she caught up with the pair, they were in a colorful garden bordered by thick, green boxwood that twisted and turned into delightful mazes, perfect for a boy to explore.

A small, open area contained a wrought iron bench next to a fanciful wishing well.

"We should have our next picnic here, Miss Sara," Nico

called. He was bent at the waist peering into the well. Sara's heart jumped into her throat.

"Nico, be careful!" Supporting her side, she broke into a run.

"Do not fear," Mr. Chang called, stepping up to balance the boy. "The well is perfectly safe."

"It's only for wishes," Nico said, looking up with a grin.

Sara breathed a sigh of relief. Though the stone and timber exterior appeared as ancient as the castle, the interior had been modernized to a solid surface pool of very shallow, crystal water.

"Papa says when he was a boy his papa brought him here to make wishes. And all his wishes came true."

Sara laughed. "He must have been a very spoiled child."

"Ah, but my wishes were always altruistic." Aleks's amused voice came from behind.

Troublesome heart doing a happy-dance, Sara whirled toward the prince. The usual tension was absent from his expression. His meeting must have gone well.

"Do you mean to say," she asked, smiling, "that you never, ever wished for anything selfish?"

"Never ever." He placed a hand on Nico's head. The boy clung to his father's knees, his face raised in adoration. "Unless you count the pony." Aleks grinned. "And perhaps the sailboat."

Sara laughed, feeling light and giddy in a way she only felt when Aleks was around. "I have no doubt you were the most indulged child in Carvainia."

"Indulged but disciplined. My father thought, and rightly so, that a crown prince could not learn to rule well if he was pampered and self-focused."

"Your father sounds like a wise man."

"A wise and strong monarch, as well as a good father. I hope to emulate him with my own son."

"You are," she said simply and received an intense look for her efforts. Did he think she hadn't noticed? "You must miss your father a lot."

He tilted his head. "I do indeed. Often I wish I could talk to him again, to seek his advice on troubling matters."

Expression pensive, he gazed toward the verdant woods. With a pinch of guilt, Sara wondered if she was one of those troubling matters.

Nico tapped Aleks's thigh. "You told your wish, Papa! Now it won't come true."

Aleks's expression lightened as he exchanged an indulgent look with Sara. "Ah, the rules of wishing. I forgot. Did you make a wish?"

"Yes, but I won't tell." The boy clamped his lips shut and slapped a palm over them.

"Excellent. A wise prince keeps his own counsel."

If Nico had any inkling what his father meant, he didn't show it. Like any little boy, his attention was snagged by a butterfly and he gave chase.

"He seems well today," Aleks said, eyes following his son.

Sara wondered if he was subtly telling her that her suspicions about Maria were nothing but fantasy, but not wanting another argument, she didn't broach the topic. Nico had not suffered any further mysterious bouts of illness, and that's really all she cared about.

"Yes. Much better, I think. No complaints, though his energy doesn't last long."

To prove the point, Nico abandoned his butterfly chase to flop wearily onto the bench.

"Are you tired now, son?" Aleks touched the rounded shoulders. Nico's breath came in small pants as though the effort of a few seconds had cost him.

He held a forefinger and thumb an inch apart. "Only a bit."

"Perhaps you and Mr. Chang should return home for a rest."

Mr. Chang, who had been standing with arms folded over his chest, moved to take Nico's hand.

By now, Nico's fatigue was as visible as his reluctance to go inside. "But Sara hasn't seen the maze. I promised."

Aleks crouched in front of the boy. "Would it be all right if I kept that promise for you? I can show Sara the maze while you rest."

Sara couldn't have been more shocked. Aleks had never willingly spent a moment alone with her. What was going on with him today?

Nico contemplated for only a moment before nodding. "I want to show her the secret passage."

"Another time perhaps. I'll save it for you."

"Okay."

After a quick hug to both Aleks and Sara, Nico followed Mr. Chang back down the long path toward the castle entrance.

Aleks watched his son depart, expression pensive. "He's taken with you."

Sara didn't know how to respond. Aleks, no doubt, was second-guessing his decision to allow her access to Nico in the first place. He'd wanted only a body part, a donor who would come and go anonymously. He'd never expected this, just as he'd never believed she cared for her baby boy. And now the evidence was mounting. Or at least she hoped it was.

Aleks had never expected, either, that Nico would intuitively respond to the woman who'd given him birth. Part of her was thrilled. Part of her worried. How would the little prince react when she left? Had she been selfish to involve herself in the child's life, knowing she couldn't stay?

She had no answers. Only the ruler of Carvainia had that

power. She longed to discuss it with him, but his reaction at the picnic had cut deep. In her precarious situation, she didn't want to risk angering him enough to send her away.

Suddenly, Aleks grabbed her hand. "Come. I promised to show you the maze."

She resisted, uncertain. "You don't have to."

"I always keep my promises."

To his son maybe. Not to her. But she didn't say that either. The prince was in a merry mood and fool that she was, she wanted to enjoy it. Tomorrow he might freeze her out again.

They started through the twisty, turning maze, coming to dead ends and half paths that led nowhere or turned back on themselves.

At one juncture where the path split in two different directions, he said, "Choose a path. Both lead out of the maze."

Sara gazed down the paths and saw nothing but dark, lush green. "I'll take that one."

"Shall we race?" he asked. "I'll take this way. You take that."

Adrenaline kicked in. "What do I get if I win?"

He looked down at her, eyes glittering. "To the victor go the spoils."

Whatever that meant.

Without waiting for a signal, she yelled, "Go!" and hurried off.

Laughing at his yelp of surprise, Sara disappeared into the narrow maze. Blood pumping with excitement, she missed a turn and had to backtrack. After only a minute, her side ached and she slowed. She'd almost forgotten about the recent surgery. But slowing down proved to be the key to noticing the subtle signs of passage. In a short time she found the exit and stepped into the sunlight.

She looked around the clearing, listening for Aleks, but

hearing only birdsong and the gentle buzz of honeybees. Seconds passed before he exited the opposite side.

Sara clapped her hands with glee. "I won. I won."

Pretending anger, Aleks stalked toward her with a growl. "I cry foul. You cheated, starting before me."

"Sorry." She giggled, breathless from the run and from his nearness. "Well, not really."

"Off with your head." Like an old-time villain, he pumped both eyebrows. If he'd had a mustache, he probably would have twirled it. "Or better yet, into the dungeon."

This was the Aleks she'd fallen in love with. This was her Aleks, unpredictable, but teasing and fun to be with.

Head back, Sara laughed, the sudden infusion of happiness a stunning, but welcome thing. He was the most complicated, confusing man, but no one else had ever made her blood hum and her skin tingle in quite this way.

She tossed her head, feeling the swirl of hair around her face. "Castles don't have dungeons these days."

"Ah, but some do." Aleks reached to brush away a stray curl and stepped closer. Sara shivered at his feather-touch. "This is an ancient castle, you know."

"Truly?" she said in disbelief, blaming her breathless voice on the race through the maze.

"Truly." He was only inches away, and every cell in her body went on full alert, yearning toward this man who had broken her heart. She was truly a fool.

"Shall I show you?" he asked, eyes twinkling with mischief and a hint of danger. "Do you dare enter the dark and terrible dungeon of Castle-by-the-Sea?"

A tingle of nervous awareness danced down her arms. "Are you trying to scare me?"

His eyes narrowed, but went right on twinkling with

mischief. "Are you game? You've explored the maze. Will you also explore the dungeon?"

She patted her heart, nervous but excited, adrenaline revved just to be with Aleks. "Are you going to lock me inside and throw away the key?"

"Are you brave enough to find out?" He laughed and the sound was so like the Aleks she'd loved, she laughed, too.

She yanked at his hand. "Come on, tough guy. I'm not afraid of the big bad wolf. Or his dungeon."

Aleks laughed again, only this time he added a wolfish growl.

A shiver ran down her back, but it was not a shiver of dread.

When they reached the castle, Aleks led the way around to an entrance Sara had never noticed before. He punched a code into an ironically modern security system and a door slowly swung open. They entered an ornately decorated hall-way, similar to those elsewhere in the castle.

"Nothing here looks creepy," she said, torn between disappointment and relief.

Aleks's look was enigmatic as he keyed in yet another security code and part of one stone wall swung inward, creaking just a bit. Musty, much cooler air wafted out.

"Okay, maybe that was creepy." Fresh shivers tingled her spine.

"You might as well get the full experience. After you, madam." The prince bowed slightly and indicated she enter.

"Oh, no, you first. I might faint if that door shut behind me."

"I thought you weren't afraid of the big bad wolf." His grin was lupine.

She thrust out her chin. "The big bad wolf I can handle." She hoped. "But the hidden door and that long dark passage-way is another matter."

With a soft chuckle, Aleks stepped around her to enter the passage. Torch holders and candle sconces had been built into the stone walls, but from what she could see there wasn't a light switch anywhere.

"Oops, we'll have to go back." She turned, half pretending to leave. "No lights."

Aleks caught her arm. "We keep a torch here."

"Torch or torture?" she asked.

One eyebrow quirked. "Dare we find out?"

She swatted his hand. "You're trying to scare me."

"Of course. What fun would it be otherwise?" From somewhere in the darkness he produced a flashlight and snapped it on, holding it beneath his chin for macabre effect.

She made a face. "Typical male."

They stepped inside and the heavy door creaked shut. The torch cast a yellow circle of light before them but scarcely illuminated the close stone walls on either side. All Sara could see was empty darkness down a long tunnel. A shiver of fear prickled the hair on the back of her neck, but it was a fun kind of fear, similar to visiting a carnival spook house.

"Five steps down," Aleks said, squeezing the hand he held, his voice hushed now in a way that made her shivers more pronounced. He was playing the part to the hilt. "Beware of loose stone—and the occasional human bone."

She squeaked, to Aleks's obvious delight, and grabbed onto his powerful upper arm. "Were prisoners really kept down here?"

He turned his head slightly and in a stage whisper asked, "Why are you whispering?"

She giggled nervously. "Good question. Were they?"

"In times past."

"None lately?"

Aleks pumped his eyebrows. "None until today."

She whacked his rock-hard arm and listened to his chuckle as they took the steps down to an enormous barred door.

"This is so cool," she whispered. "Just like in storybooks."

"I doubt the original occupants saw the charm." Aleks shone the flashlight around so she could get a better look. The space was, indeed, an ancient dungeon, dark, damp, cold and lonely. "This same gate has been here since the pits were dug in the sixteen hundreds. Before that, prisoners were housed in the towers of the castle keep."

"Fascinating. It's like walking back in time. Do you have a key to this door?"

"Of course." He reached above the door, scratching around until he came up with a huge skeleton key which he used to unlock the heavy iron door. Its clang echoed eerily off the rocks. Sara shuddered, imagining the fear a captive would have experienced upon hearing that hopeless sound.

Another set of narrow, stone steps took them down deeper into the cold belly of the castle. The darkness increased as did the damp smell.

"The air smells like the old storm cellars in Kansas. Musty and dirty. Do you come down here often?"

He shook his head. "Not since I was a boy and got lost in one of the passageways."

"Lost? You mean there is more than one tunnel?"

"Many. The maze in the gardens is nothing compared to this one. In ancient times, captives went crazy thinking they could escape only to find themselves forever lost in the tunnels. Such was the plan of the builders, an elemental and effective form of torture."

"Eww. Horrid." She stood in the center of a small stone room, rubbing the chill from her crossed arms. "How did you get out?"

"My father and half the royal army searched for hours.

After that, Father closed off most of the tunnels, filled in the death pits and placed a small window up there." He aimed the flashlight upward. "Though it gives only a little light, anyone who knows where to look can see down into any open section of the dungeon."

"No more lost boys."

"Hopefully not."

"Will you ever bring Nico down here?"

"Eventually. This is his heritage. He must understand where he came from before he can decide where to lead his people."

Sara didn't say the obvious. Nico had also come from her. Half his heritage was a world away from Carvainia's beautiful shores. Shouldn't he understand that part of himself, as well?

But she didn't voice the question. Aleks had been crystal clear on the topic.

Instead, she slowly twirled around, taking in her surroundings. "Is it safe to explore?"

"As long as you have a guide." He lowered his voice to a spooky whisper. "Though beware. The place is haunted and the cries of the tortured can be heard on moonlit nights."

"Stop it," she said, laughing though a bit nervously.

By now, her eyes had adjusted to the dimness and Sara began to move around, morbidly fascinated by the dungeon and its beastly history. The chamber was small and narrow with stone ledges built around the walls and divots here and there in the rock. Though she didn't know their purposes, she could imagine men lying on the ledges to avoid the rats and filth. The divots were a puzzle.

Like dark and deathly fingers, passageways led off in several directions from the central room so she could fully comprehend the false hope of escape. She shuddered to think of the real people who had perished in this place.

She was studying yet another wall divot when Aleks touched her arm. She jumped and spun around, bumping into his chest. Without thinking, she latched on like a frightened child, pulling him tight. He wrapped both arms around her.

"A bit edgy, aren't you?" A soft laugh rumbled against her ear.

Embarrassed by her reaction, she started to pull away. He held her for moment longer and then stepped back, his face unreadable in the shadowy light.

Sara turned her face aside, heart thudding for far more reasons than fear of the dungeon.

"It *is* creepy down here." Stirred by the strength and nearness of Aleks she moved away to touch a place in the wall. "What is this?"

A beat of silence passed. She could feel Aleks behind her, but she could not read his thoughts. Did he suspect her emotional turmoil? Did he realize how confused and troubled she felt because of him? Did he know what power he wielded over her? Not only the power to keep her from Nico, but the power to break her heart all over again.

After a bit, he lightly touched her elbow. "Come. I'll show you." His voice held a strained note that she didn't understand.

Saying little, they journeyed out of the central chamber down a tunnel so low they had to crouch and their bodies pressed close. Sara had never been more aware of Aleks's size and strength than she was in that tunnel.

Once, she bumped her elbow and an involuntary gasp of pain hissed out. Aleks maneuvered her to his front, spooning his body around hers.

She felt strangely, wonderfully protected as he guided her through the tunnel.

Too quickly, the moment was over. They stepped out into

a second, larger chamber and separated. Sara felt the loss clear to her cold feet.

Seemingly unaffected, Aleks shone the torch around the walls.

"Here you go," he murmured. "These are still intact. The ones in the anteroom were removed before my time."

Rings of iron hung in pairs at the top and bottom all around the room. Here and there, a piece of heavy chain still dangled from the rings.

"Stocks?" she asked, gruesomely fascinated.

At Aleks's nod, Sara went to one pair and stretched her hands up to grasp the rings. "Like this?"

"If you were a prisoner, would you want to face the hard stone?"

"Probably not." She turned to face him, leaning her back into the wall while grasping the rings above her head. "Would I get a choice?"

"Good point." One hand on his hip, he cocked his head. "I think I like this."

"What? Me in stocks?"

"Hmm. Definitely." He came closer.

Sara dipped her chin, feeling saucy and tingly. "Why? So you can control my every move?"

A slight smile tugged at the corner of his mouth. "Now, that would be a wondrous ability. Nothing more to worry about."

Certain he meant the situation with Nico, Sara was insulted. She started to step away.

Aleks blocked her. "Not so fast. I've been thinking…"

Her heart began to hammer, but most definitely not from fear or insult. Aleks's dark eyes held no animosity, no hostility. What she saw there was powerful male desire.

A responding ache settled low in her belly.

Her tongue flicked out nervously. "Thinking about what? Taking me prisoner in your dungeon?"

"I should have considered it sooner." Eyes teasing, lips curved, he moved closer, trapping her against the stone wall. She couldn't have moved if she'd wanted to. And she certainly did not want to.

A sexy, passionate prince was irresistible. Even in a dungeon.

He slid his hands upward along the length of her bare arms. When he reached her fingers, he twined his with hers. His warrior's body, firm and sleek, pressed into hers. Goose bumps followed in the wake of his touch. She shivered, deliciously.

He noticed. His nostrils flared.

"You are torturing me, Sara Presley," he murmured, his mouth close enough to brush hers in a tantalizing tickle.

With a soft laugh, Sara said, "I think you'd better look again, Prince Charming. I'm the one held captive."

Did that breathless, sexy voice belong to her?

"What shall we do about this?" he murmured. "What shall we do?"

Sara had no answer. They could never return to their carefree youth, nor could they move forward with no trust between them. No matter how attracted she was, her heart remembered the long, lonely years after he'd left. Regardless of his excuses, he *had* left her. And he had not returned.

If Nico hadn't fallen ill, Aleks would never have contacted her. He would have forever kept her son a secret.

How could she forgive him for that?

Yet, she'd been the one to give away their child. His loathing was not without reason.

She sighed. The dilemma had no resolution. She could not change what was.

She studied the strong lines of his aristocratic face and

knew she desired him, but more than this, she still loved the man inside the handsome body. What kind of crazy woman continued to love a man who hated her?

Or did he?

The emotion emanating from the prince was not loathing. It was desire.

Was desire enough?

"Aleks," she murmured, every nerve in her body more alive than she'd been in years.

He shook his head slightly, his rapid breath fanning her cheek. "Shh. Shh."

His heart pounded against hers. Two hearts beating. One restrained, the other yearning but afraid to trust again, afraid to hope.

Tension pulsated from Aleks in waves. He wanted her but he didn't want to want her.

Sara experienced a rush of power in that sudden realization. She longed to break through that control of his, to force him to be *her* Aleks again even for a moment.

Though she would willingly remain trapped against the wall for as long as Aleks was here, the hard, irregular stone was cold against her back. Aleks, on the other hand, exuded heat.

"Are you going to kiss me or kill me?" she murmured, so close to his mouth that she could have made the first move if she'd wanted to. But she wouldn't. She might be the captive, but Aleks needed to surrender.

"So impatient," he whispered, but one hand slid down to stroke her cheek. She shivered. He smiled. She turned her head to one side. He brought it back to center and traced her mouth with one finger.

"Arrogant pig," she said.

"Tempting wench."

She nipped at his finger. He laughed softly, dark eyes glittering like onyx, as he finally, finally touched his lips to hers.

He was worth the wait.

A shock of sensation washed through her like a tidal wave. She twisted free from his grip, wanting, needing to touch him. With both arms, she clasped him to her, reveling in his power and maleness.

When Aleks felt her response, he dropped his hold to thread his fingers through her hair, capturing her more completely with his kiss than he ever could with stocks and chains.

She murmured softly, feeling the hum of yearning take control. It was as though her whole being had been in a state of suspension, waiting for her prince to come along and bring her back to life.

She wanted the moment to never end. Reality had problems neither she nor Aleks knew how to resolve. But here, in his dungeon hideaway, she could forget all of that, forget the reasons they could not be together, forget the years of heartbreak.

When the kiss ended, far sooner than she'd have liked, Aleks didn't move away. He kissed her nose, her eyelids, her forehead before resting his face in her hair. His strident breathing matched her own. She could feel the powerful beat of the pulse in his throat.

For a while, they remained still; both seemed satisfied just to hold the other.

Aware now that she had one arm around his waist and another around his neck, she let her fingers trace the coarse outline of hair at his nape and gloried in his soft murmur of pleasure.

Did the tough warrior prince never experience tenderness?

The thought touched her to the core. Someone as strong as Aleks never wanted to exhibit a perceived weakness. He would deny himself the most basic emotional needs to remain strong and in control.

She stroked the back of his neck and traced the lean shape of his jaw.

His eyes dropped shut. Sara kissed them. A smile lifted the corners of his mouth.

"You smell good," he said, inhaling deeply.

"Like a cold, damp dungeon?"

The smile widened. "Like a soft, warm woman. Like sunshine and flowers. The way I remember."

The answer stunned her. "You remember?"

"Always." The admission seemed to bother him.

"You never told me." Silence and secrets had cost her everything. "Why didn't you tell me?"

"Were compliments that important to you?"

"I'm not talking about compliments and you know it."

His whole body stiffened. She felt his withdrawal long before he pulled back from touching her. And when he did, the chilled air rushed in to fill the space. She crossed her arms, afraid now that she'd spoiled their afternoon.

"You were the one with secrets."

"We both made mistakes—"

He cut her off with a slice of his hand. "Don't talk to me of mistakes. My son is not a mistake."

"I didn't mean—" She reached for him. He backed away.

"Come. Security will be concerned."

The return trip through the tunnels was made in silent regret. Sara wondered why she couldn't keep her mouth shut.

# CHAPTER EIGHT

"YOUR MAJESTY? SIR? Prince Aleksandre?"

A hand touched his arm and Aleks jerked to attention. A dozen curious faces stared at him around the meeting table. Ambassadors from around the globe had gathered to discuss energy concerns, and he hadn't heard a word they'd said.

"A thousand pardons." He dipped his head. "My mind wandered."

Sara had bewitched him. He could think of nothing but her taste and scent and the way she'd melded against him as though she were part of him. Last night, he'd slept little and when he did, a red-haired woman tortured him with kisses and lies.

The ambassador from Great Britain frowned in sympathy from the far end of the table. "How is your son?"

Though ashamed to use Nico as his excuse, Aleks answered, "Much better, thank you. He's encountered some rejection issues but for the most part is recovering well at present."

"Excellent. You have our kind regards."

"Thank you. And again my apologies. Shall we address the next item on the agenda?"

The company returned to the issues at hand, haggling over a variety of concerns. He reached for his pad of paper. Note-taking should keep him focused. To his dismay, doodles filled one side of the page. Doodles of flowers and handcuffs. His thoughts turned again to Sara, to their afternoon together. What was he going to do about Sara Presley?

When the meeting finally adjourned, Aleks had no idea what had been decided.

An hour later, he stepped into Nico's playroom, fully expecting—and if he was honest, hoping—to face the tormenting woman. She wasn't there. A disturbing tremor of disappointment passed through him.

Nico jumped up from a small chair and ran to him. He enveloped his son in a hug, holding back the question pressing on his tongue. Where was Sara?

The attending nurse, Maria, dipped into a curtsy. Behind her, a small table was set with several open jars and a loaf of bread.

"Your Majesty. What a pleasant surprise." Carlo's mother smiled as though delighted to greet him. As always, seeing her brought memories of the man who'd saved his life.

"And I am delighted to see you." He took her hand, raised it to his lips. "How is the mother of Carvainia's finest soldier?"

Sadness flickered through her eyes. She glanced away. "I am faring quite well, thanks to your generosity."

"It is nothing." He could not bring back her son but he could give her a home and a place of respect within his court. Carlo would be pleased, though Aleks's regret would never be assuaged.

"Where is Mr. Chang?" he asked.

"He was called away."

"His duty is here. I do not want Prince Nico left alone."

Maria's dark eyes registered hurt. "Sir, do you not trust me, the mother of your best friend and most loyal servant, to care for our prince? I have no son of my own now. The young prince has become my life and soul. Surely, you know that."

Guilt punched him in the gut. "Of course. I meant nothing except that Chang must not shirk his responsibility."

She inclined her head in acceptance. "I'm sure he will return shortly. Would you care to join us in our snack?"

"Yes, Papa, please." Nico bracketed his father's face with both hands. Aleks's heart lifted in his chest. "We're having an American original. Peanut butter and jelly. I have never tasted anything so grand."

Aleks chuckled. "And who told you about this delicacy?"

"Miss Sara. Her friend sent it all the way from America just for me. She said all little boys in America love PB and J."

It was the perfect opening. "Where is Miss Sara today?"

Nico's thin shoulders arched. "I don't know. She brought the peanut butter and went away again."

"In her suite with Dr. Konstantine, I believe, sir," Maria answered. As she spoke, she lovingly stroked Nico's hair with her fingers. Nico looked up at her with happy eyes.

The woman adored Nico. Any fool could see that. He was the son she no longer had.

The knowledge eased the worry nagging in the back of his mind. Nico was safe with Maria. Sara was wrong.

"Is Miss Presley unwell?" he asked.

Marie gazed at him with curiosity. Had she noticed the tension in his voice?

"My apologies, Your Majesty. I do not know."

Aleks fidgeted, torn between Nico and Sara. Was she all right? She'd had surgery, too. Had she overdone yesterday in their race through the maze? Or had he pushed her too hard, holding her captive against the cold wall? Was she injured?

The memory of those moments roared back. She had made

him laugh. She had made him feel. For those few hours, he'd forgotten the weight of a nation, the horrors of war, and he'd felt young and free again.

He spun around. "I will return soon."

"But Papa—"

Over one shoulder, he winked and said, "Save me a peanut butter sandwich."

By the time he reached Sara's suite, tension corded his neck, but another emotion plagued him, too. The need to see her was as strong. He knew she was trouble, and yet he could not seem to stay away.

He lifted a knuckle and rapped softly. If Dr. Konstantine was still present, he could apprise Aleks of Sara's condition.

Sara opened the door. His stomach dipped. Red hair flowing around her shoulders, she was barefoot in a long terry cloth robe. And she'd been crying.

An alarm went off in his head. He pushed his way inside the room. "What's wrong? Why are you crying? Are you unwell?"

She stared at him standing inside her room, fists clenched at his side, and said drily, "Come on in, Aleks. You're welcome to burst into my room at any time."

He reached behind her and closed the door. "Answer me. What's wrong?"

"Don't be imperative with me." She sniffed and brushed away a tear glistening on one cheek.

He took her shoulders. "Did I hurt you yesterday?"

She blinked. "What are you so fired up about?"

"Dr. Konstantine was here. I thought—" Beginning to feel like a fool, he shut his mouth and crushed her to his chest.

With a sigh, she settled against his shoulder. He stroked the back of her hair, loving the texture of silk against his skin.

"I'm fine, Aleks," she murmured, her mouth dangerously close to his neck. He felt the softness of her lips as they moved against the stiff collar of his shirt. If he moved his head just a little, she would be kissing him.

"Then why was Dr. Konstantine here?"

"An exam. That's all." But her voice quivered as she spoke.

He pushed her a little away, but was reluctant to turn her loose. She seemed fragile today, not at all her usual feisty self.

"Then why are you trembling?"

She shook her head. "No reason. All is well. Please."

She tried turning away, but he drew her back to him.

"Come. Let's sit down. You are shaky and we need to talk."

"That's a first. You, the king of silence, want to talk."

"Prince," he corrected with a slight smile. "Not king."

Her smile returned, watery and weak, but at least present.

He led the way to a settee in the living space of her suite. She sat down and curled her feet beneath her, pedicured toes peeking out from her long robe.

"That color becomes you," he said, nodding toward her feet.

She lifted her hands to display fingernails in the same pale shade. "Your staff is exceptional. I've never been so pampered in my life." Again, tears sprang to her eyes. She dashed them away with the sleeve of her robe.

"What has upset you, Sara?" Aleks moved closer on the settee, knees turned toward her, aching to touch her again, and not sure what she needed. Why would the mention of a manicure bring tears?

"Is there something else you need that is not being provided?" Heads would roll if anyone had disobeyed his orders.

"Oh, Aleks, don't you know? Don't you get it?" She turned her face away, her delicate profile tragic as tears slid down on her cheeks.

He stopped resisting and touched her, using the tips of his fingers to wipe away her tears. "Was I too rough in the dungeon? Did I ask too much of you in the maze? Are you injured?"

Her look was indulgent as though he was a dim-witted child. "Yesterday was…wonderful."

Her admission forced the words from him. "I thought so, too."

"But you got angry again. You walked away." She grasped his hands, leaning toward him, her face earnest. "Couldn't we just this once have a conversation the way we used to? Could we please forget everything that's come between and just be honest with each other?"

Unease quivered in his belly. Did the woman know the meaning of honesty? Was this merely a skillful maneuver to get her way?

"What would you like to discuss?"

"Anything, everything except the hurt we've caused each other. Talk to me of your work, your vineyards, your boats. Let me know you again. Help me know my son. Tell me about him as a baby. When did he take his first steps? When did he get his first tooth?"

As a leader and strategist, he prided himself on being able to read the intent of others. In Sara's sea-colored eyes, he saw no hidden deceit, only longing. She had missed Nico's infancy. Yes, the fault was her own, but she had suffered for it. There could be no harm in sharing memories of their son.

And so he talked. Occasionally, she interrupted with a question, a laugh, a touch. When the topic of Nico was exhausted, they moved on to memories of each other. The time she sobbed so loudly at a sad movie that he'd grown embarrassed. The time she'd baked him a lopsided birthday cake.

"You ate every bite."

"It was delicious." He had long since relaxed into the sofa, his legs stretched out before him. Sara had always had the ability to take away his worries and make him relax. Even then, he'd had the troubles of a nation on his mind, and though she hadn't known, she'd had a soothing influence on him.

"Really?" she asked, grinning. "Then I'll ask the chef to let me bake another just for you."

With a laugh, he pulled her to him, resting her head on his shoulder. She fit well as though her curves were made for him.

He sighed, a gusty sound. What was he going to do about Sara Presley? She was under his roof and in his mind all the time. And she challenged everything he knew to be true. At least where their son was concerned.

Desire swamped him and he kissed her, reveling in the sweet way her arms snaked around his neck and in the way only Sara could make him feel.

As much as he despised the weakness, he was irresistibly drawn to this woman who'd given him Nico.

Desire. Yes, it must be desire, for that was the only emotion he could allow himself to feel for Sara Presley. He let himself wonder if he dared take her for a mistress. If he did, would he ever be able to let her go?

Sara leaned on the door facing and watched Aleks's lean, straight back disappear into the elevator. Happiness danced in her heart. She raised a hand to well-kissed lips.

They'd spent two hours together without once fighting.

Granted, they had not discussed their hot button topic, but still, they'd communicated. Today gave her hope.

The elevator pinged, taking Aleks away. Sara started back inside the room when a movement from the opposite end of the hall caught her attention. She turned, sure she saw the edge of an arm before it disappeared. Hair stood up on the back of her neck.

"Silly," she said. But a shadow sprawled along the floor, as if someone stood against the wall, just out of sight.

Why would anyone do that? Was it a servant, aware that Aleks had been inside her room and now eager to spread the gossip? Not unlikely.

Curious, she traveled the length of the hall. As she approached the shadow withdrew. Turning the corner, she saw no one.

The short hall opened into a stairwell on one side and into the exercise room on the other. She peeked through the small observation window. A man in shorts and tennis shoes pumped madly on a stationary bicycle. He glanced up, raising an eyebrow.

Sara gave an embarrassed wave. She wasn't the only guest in this wing, though she seldom saw the others.

The man nodded and went back to his sweat and bicycling.

Unable to shake the creepy feeling that someone had been spying on her—or maybe Aleks—Sara considered taking the stairs down. As she placed one hand on the cool knob, she chided herself as being silly.

The shadow must have belonged to a servant. Castle servants, as she'd already discovered, loved to carry gossip. No reason to see intrigue around every corner.

Wrapping her robe tighter, she padded barefoot back to her room. Aleks's expensive, subtle cologne lingered in the air. She breathed it in, wondering if they could find their way to each other again.

During his visit, they had shared a cup of tea. The dishes remained on her table. She went to it, lifted his cup and kissed the edge where his mouth had been.

Was there any way she could ever repay the mistake she'd

made? Was there any hope that he could forgive her? And that she could forgive him? Today she almost believed it could happen.

But time was short.

Tears prickled the back of her eyelids. Aleks had thought she was crying from discomfort. She'd been afraid to tell him the truth. That Dr. Konstantine had pronounced her fit enough to travel soon. Very soon.

Her time with Nico, and with Aleks, was running out.

"Nico."

She hurried to the closet and began to dress. Though she had hope, Aleks could very well send her away with nothing. Every moment with her son was precious.

In ten minutes flat, her sandals made soft click-click sounds on the carpeted corridor of the family wing. She shook her head in wonder that a child of hers would have an entire suite to himself. The playroom, where he now spent much of his time, was a wonderland of toys and equipment. A climbing toy and tube slide occupied one side of the big room. Colorful game rugs, blocks, a train, electronics, books, art supplies and shelves of toys filled the space.

He son had everything…except his mother.

Eager to tell Nico about the flock of feeding cranes she'd seen from her balcony, she sailed inside the playroom without knocking…and came up short.

Nico played at a sand table.

The nurse Maria stood at his side, a glass in hand that she was offering to Nico.

Her little prince took the drink and sipped.

Sara's stomach hurt. Why was Maria here, alone, with her son? But she knew the answer. Aleks had considered her concerns as nothing more than hysteria. Or manipulation.

She must have made a sound because Maria turned, smiling. "Miss Presley, welcome."

"Sara, Sara!" Nico handed the glass to Maria and rushed to Sara.

As she went to her haunches to embrace her son, Sara watched Maria over Nico's shoulder. The woman looked on, a fond expression on her face.

Maria's friendliness made Sara feel ridiculous. Maybe there was no connection between Nico's bouts of vomiting and this particular nurse. After all, Maria was with him every day. If the nurse had an ulterior motive, wouldn't Nico be sick more often?

Perhaps she was imagining things. Perhaps the stress and emotional turmoil of recent weeks had stolen her common sense.

Much later, when Nico had grown tired enough for a rest, Sara made her way back to the guest suite. Dinner would be served soon and she wanted to relax in the spa tub first and consider today's events. Once she returned to Kansas, there would be no more servants, no more spa treatments, no more candle-lined hot tub.

Not that she craved any of those things, but they were nice.

After Antonia filled the private tub, lit the candles and sprinkled fragrant bath salts into the water, she left a tray of fruit and mineral water on the edge and slipped out of the room.

Sara took her cell phone and settled into the steaming water. She made a habit of calling Penny every night. Her friend, though furious at Aleks, remained enamored of the "royal treatment" as she termed Sara's experience in the castle. So, to please her friend, Sara kept her worries to herself and told story after story about the beautiful castle and luxurious treatments.

Using her big toe, she pressed the jet button and slid down into the swirling water as she punched in the long-distance numbers.

She and Penny chatted for a while, laughing above the noise of the tub. Sara told her about the maze and the dungeon, but kept the kisses to herself.

"You sound happier today," Penny said.

"I'm feeling better."

"No, it's more than that. I've known you a long time, girl-friend. You sound different."

"I've found my son."

"Yes, but you found him weeks ago. What's going on? Tell Aunt Penny."

Sara chuckled. "Stop prying. I'll tell you when I come home."

"Are you falling for that prince jerk again?"

Sara couldn't answer without lying.

Penny groaned through the receiver. "Sara, honey, be careful. He hurt you before. He'll do it again."

Wasn't that what she feared?

"Don't worry about me." She tried to sound breezy. "I'm having the time of my life. Servants, massages, pedicures. You should see my toenails."

Penny said no more but Sara knew her friend was worried. So was she.

After the call ended, a thoughtful Sara placed the phone on the edge of the tub and leaned her head back. She needed to get out soon before she was wrinkled as a raisin.

As she silenced the jetting tub, she heard a noise. She sat up, listening. The walls in this place were too thick to hear through. Was someone in her suite?

"Antonia?"

No answer.

Frowning, she exited the tub, dried quickly and slipped into the thick robe, pulling it close around her. Aleks had toyed with the belt of this robe earlier today. It was the first time since coming here that she'd considered what it would be like to make love with him again.

Dangerous thoughts, to be sure.

She padded out of the bath into the living space and found it empty.

Her imagination was playing tricks on her today.

A knock sounded on her door.

Like a lovesick teenager, her mind immediately thought of Aleks.

She rushed to the door and opened it.

Looking down her aristocratic nose with disapproval was Queen Irena.

# CHAPTER NINE

"YOUR HIGHNESS." Not well versed on the proper way to address a Queen Mother, Sara dipped in a half curtsy.

The queen arched one brow. "Miss Presley. May I come in?"

How did she refuse a royal? She didn't. She and the handsome queen had been introduced, but the woman had never before made a point of starting a conversation. On the contrary, Queen Irena had hiked her nose and hurried away every time they met. It didn't take a genius to figure out that she disapproved of her grandson's mother.

Sara opened the door wider and the queen swept inside with the air of one accustomed to being in charge and having her way.

Like mother, like son.

The thought amused Sara, but she didn't smile. She was far too uncomfortable in the queen's presence. What could the woman possibly want?

Eyes so like Aleks's swept around the room before coming to rest on Sara.

"I trust you are well." Rather than a kindness, the words sounded like a command.

"Yes."

"Excellent. Then I expect you shall be leaving us soon. May I enquire as to when that might be?"

Sara blinked, stunned by the obvious effort to get rid of her. "I—I—I'm not sure yet."

The queen looked disappointed but was undaunted. "I'll be happy to have my secretary make the arrangements. How would tomorrow be?"

"Tomorrow?"

"Surely, you see the reason behind leaving as soon as possible? The longer you remain in Prince Domenico's company, the more difficult the parting will be." She offered a smile that never reached her eyes. "Especially for the child. Our prince is too fragile for emotional upheavals, don't you agree?"

"Yes, of course, but—"

"Wonderful. I will send my secretary to you, and let Antonia know to prepare your belongings for travel right away."

"No!"

The queen looked taken aback. "I beg your pardon?"

"I'm not leaving tomorrow."

"But you must."

"I can't." Grasping for a reason to stay, Sara latched onto a thin hope. "Dr. Konstantine has not yet released me medically."

"I see." The queen's nostrils flared, but she kept her composure. "Very well, then. But do keep me informed as to your plans. I want very much to accommodate you in every way possible. We are ever so grateful for all you've done."

Right. That's why she was so eager to have Sara gone. But this was Aleks's mother, Nico's grandmother, and Sara would be civil even when deeply offended by the woman's carefully worded rudeness.

"Helping Nico has been one of the greatest joys of my life."

One side of Queen Irena's mouth twisted. "How kind of you."

The words were polite but her expression was nothing short of hostile.

"Not kind, Your Highness," Sara said. "Love. I'm his mother. I love him."

Queen Irena seemed to weigh a response but in the end, chose to switch strategies. That she disliked Sara was obvious. Apparently, Aleks had poisoned her mind with his anger, and there was nothing Sara could do about it. To all the royal family except Nico, she was the evil American who had abandoned the heir to a throne.

The fact that they were correct didn't help one bit.

"I saw Prince Aleksandre leave your rooms."

Ah, now they were getting somewhere. But Sara was not about to satisfy the woman's curiosity, particularly now, when she and Aleks seemed to be opening up to each other. The relationship was far too fragile to share.

If Queen Irena wanted to know why her son had been in this suite, she would have to ask him.

When Sara kept silent, the queen said, "Did His Majesty mention the grand affair coming up this weekend?"

"No." That she was not privy to such details of his life pained her.

"Of course not. Why would he? It is a royal affair that has nothing to do with you."

Sara tried not to let the words affect her, but her insides trembled. "Why indeed."

"Diplomats from around the region will be dining and dancing in the Grand Ballroom."

"How nice." Sara was not an idiot. She knew very well she did not fit into this lifestyle, but Queen Irena seemed intent on forcing the issue.

"I wouldn't want to—how shall I put this delicately—

offend Prince Aleksandre's fiancée. She doesn't know of your *previous* relationship and we can't have her upset."

Sara felt the blood drain from her face. Her body went numb. "I didn't know Aleks was engaged."

"Well, not officially yet, but very soon. I wouldn't expect you to know anything about that. How could you, not being privy to the inner workings of royalty. Marriages in our class are always among our own kind. Aleksandre has known Duchess Philamena since they both were small children. They've been in love for years. She will make a wonderful queen to my son."

But he'd kissed *her*. He'd fathered a child with *her*. Did his fiancée know that?

Of course she didn't, which was exactly why Queen Irena was here. She wanted Sara out of the way, fearful that a plain bookshop owner from Kansas could shake the royal family tree.

Sara wanted to laugh hysterically. Or maybe she wanted to weep.

She was a nobody from Kansas who didn't even know who her father was. Aleks was a prince with a pedigree as long as history. She was nothing but a fling who had surprised him with a child.

And yet, he'd come to her today. He'd expressed caring and concern. They'd laughed and touched and kissed. He felt passion for her, she was certain.

But did he feel anything more?

According to Queen Irena, he did not. He could not.

Regardless of these last few days of hopefulness, Prince Aleksandre was completely out of her league.

If only she could accept it and let him go.

* * *

Humming softly, Aleks tucked the photograph album under one arm as he stepped off the elevator. Earlier when he and Sara had talked, Sara had eagerly soaked up every scrap of information he shared about Nico. It had occurred to him this afternoon, in the middle of a news conference, that she had never seen any photos of her son as an infant.

He paused, staring down at the crested album. He'd referred to Nico as her son. Odd. When had he switched loyalties? When had he come to think of Sara as Nico's mother?

Concern fluttered under his ribs like a case of indigestion.

He'd never fully listened to her side of the story. Part of him wanted to, but he'd spent so many years despising her, blaming her, he was afraid of her lies.

What if she hadn't lied?

The elevator doors rumbled open.

But she had. He was certain. His mother had told him of Sara's treachery. Mother would know. She'd been there.

He gripped the photo album tighter. He and Sara had shared a pleasant interlude. That was all. Nothing serious. And she *had* given Nico new life when Aleks feared all hope was lost. She deserved this gift in return. It was the least he could do to show his gratitude.

The thought of that million-dollar contract nagged the edges of his mind. Wasn't that gratitude enough?

The conflicting ideas annoyed him. He tried to shake them off. Sara would be gone soon and none of this would matter.

A sick feeling pulled at his gut. Sara would be out of his life again.

Would this time be forever?

He wasn't ready to let her go again.

Desire. That's all it could be. He was a man, accustomed

to having women, though he was rigidly discreet. Since Nico's illness he had been celibate.

Yes, desire was as good an excuse as any for this fixation on Sara Presley.

As Aleks stepped off the elevator, his mind jumping from the reasons he should despise Sara to the reasons he shouldn't, he was surprised to observe Queen Irena coming down the corridor. She wore her usual two-piece suit, probably silk, only this one was blood-red and screamed power. Her hair, always immaculately groomed, appeared freshly coiffed. Her pumps made firm taps on the floor. He knew that walk. She was annoyed.

"Mother?" he said, curious.

Her hand went to the creamy scarf at her throat. "Aleksandre. You startled me."

Indeed. She sounded breathless.

"What are you doing in the guest wing? Has someone arrived already?" With the event planned for this weekend, he would not be surprised to find guests arriving early. Carvainia Castle was noted for its luxury treatment of all guests.

"No, I—" His mother looked extremely nervous for some reason. "I was speaking to Miss Presley."

Knowing how the queen had both ignored and avoided "that American woman," Aleks went on alert. "Sara? Why would you want to talk to Sara?"

"I wished to express my gratitude in person. She has done our country a great service."

Something in his mother's manner didn't ring true. "I see."

"Do you?" She gripped his elbow, eyes narrowed. "Why are *you* here, my son? To express your *gratitude*, as well?"

Aleksandre knew from her tone that the queen suspected more than gratitude drew him to Sara. At the moment, he couldn't say for certain if she was right or wrong. Regardless of his reasons, he would not share the information with his mother.

All he knew was that he had to see Sara.

"I do not need to explain my activities."

With a sharp gasp of hurt, she dropped her hand. "Gossip is flying, Aleksandre. You were in her rooms earlier. Now you are here again. Have you no sense where this wicked American is concerned? Does she have some sort of power over you?"

He'd wondered the same thing. "Don't be ludicrous."

"Listen to me, my son. I am not without sympathy. You are a man without a wife. You have needs, and yet as prince you bear a responsibility to be especially careful. There are Carvainian women who would welcome your attentions."

"Mother—" he started. Though his thoughts had been along similar lines, his libido was not something he cared to discuss with his mother.

She raised a hand to silence him. "Hear me. Duchess Philamena will be here this weekend as well as other beautiful women of royal blood. It is time for you to choose one of them. Take a queen. Take a mistress. But this attraction for the American is dangerous."

"Do you think I am not man enough to handle Sara Presley?"

She drew up to her full height, head high and eyes of dark fire. "You are a warrior prince, a ruler with ice in your veins and the heart of a lion. You serve your country with honor and dignity every day. Five years ago, you were young and untried. The unworthy woman turned your head and broke your heart. You are too strong, too proud and too wise to allow this to happen again."

As her lips quivered with the passion of her words, Alek saw her intent. She was not interfering. She was afraid for him

He touched her shoulder and said gently, "I will think about these things."

Seeing that she could do no more, the queen nodded once and continued her journey, leaving him in the corridor with Nico's photographs in his hand.

Mother was right in many ways.

Sara had fooled him before. He glanced toward the closed door of her suite.

Even now, after his mother's impassioned speech, the thought of being with Sara called to him like a siren's song. As long as she was under his roof, he could not stay away.

Sara awakened at dawn, inexplicably drawn to the balcony. A hill gently sloped from the castle to the seashore. A fading moon cast a silvery reflection across the water and dimly lit a solitary figure walking along the sandy beach below. Head down, hands in his pockets, he looked more than alone. He looked lonely.

What must it be like for a man so young to have such responsibility on his shoulders? Granted, Aleks was a man born and trained to the role and yet, the Aleks she'd known would care deeply, worry too much and try too hard. Failure, for Aleks d'Gabriel, was never an option.

In the last few days she'd seen more and more glimpses of the old Aleks beneath the angry face he'd first presented.

She suffered for him, wishing for a way to ease his burdens—a laughable sentiment.

"Aleks," she whispered, fingers touching the spot over her heart that called to him as eagerly as her lips.

As if he'd heard, he turned toward the castle. The sea breeze caught her hair and tossed it back, then played with the edge of her robe, baring her legs and unshod feet. She lifted a hand in greeting.

She could almost imagine Aleks's smile as he waved in return.

Heart lifting, she waved again before going to the balcony gate. The last few days had been wonderful. Though she'd battled falling in love with Aleks again, yesterday, she'd lost the fight.

Nico's baby photo album had broken down the last barrier. She'd cried, her heart aching for all she'd missed, but she'd also cried with joy that Aleks would intuitively understand how important those pictures were to her. He had held her and kissed away her tears.

Then he'd paged through the album, telling sweet stories behind each photo until she'd almost felt as if she'd been there.

Last night, she had taken dinner with him and Nico, and later, after reading a story to the little prince and tucking him in bed, the two of them had watched a movie in the theater room. Rather, the movie had played. They had not watched.

They had talked. And touched. And used the cover of darkness as an excuse for more kisses. He wanted to make love to her. She could feel it in the passion of his kiss and tremble of his body against hers. She wanted that, too, but she would not because other than renewed desire for one another, nothing had really changed. They had never resolved the terrible rift lying dormant like a volcano waiting to erupt.

Yet their attraction couldn't be denied, an attraction that, to Sara, was far more than physical. She loved him with a love that wanted what was best for him.

But what exactly was best for Aleks? A duchess he had known from birth? Or a commoner from Kansas who'd given him a son?

Beneath the austerity of his position, Aleks was still Aleks

She knew he'd suffered terribly in the war. He'd told her as much. War had changed him, hardened him, shattered his faith in humanity. He was edgier and more cautious, but he could still make her feel like the most incredible woman on earth.

Now, she rushed through the semidarkness, feeling the soft sea spray blowing in from the shore and the fine-grained sand against her feet. Aleks had turned to watch her approach.

He pulled her to him. She tiptoed up for a morning kiss.

"A princess risen from the sea to beguile me," he said, his deep voice hushed against the backdrop of rushing waves.

Smiling, her head tilted up, she asked, "Are you beguiled?"

"Completely."

The reply sent her soul soaring like the first waking seagulls. She, too, was beguiled.

He kissed her nose and then looped an arm around her waist drawing her to his side. They faced the sea and the eastern sky where the first tinges of pinks and grays heralded the coming sun. The moon turned to white and the last visible star clung to the fading night.

They were quiet for a while, absorbing the peaceful morning, content to be together. At least, Sara was content. If only there was a way to make things right so that she never had to leave this place. But the thought was useless. Even if the issues between Aleks and her were resolved, he was still a prince. And royals married royals, as his mother had so carefully pointed out.

A wave crashed against the shore, sending a mist over them. Sara drew back with a laugh, but crossed her arms against the coolness.

"You are cold?"

"No. I'm fine." More than fine. Being here with Aleks in the breaking morning filled her with a sense of completion.

Here, there was no one to interfere. There was no painful past, no argument, no feelings of loathing, no prince and pauper. Here in the darkness, they were simply Aleks and Sara.

"You shouldn't get chilled."

"I'm not, Aleks. Truly." The thought came that he might be trying to politely rid himself of her. "Unless you want me to go."

Aleks shook his head. His arm tightened around her. "Stay."

That one word warmed her as no blanket could. "I can see why you come to the beach at dawn. There's a serenity here."

"You feel it, too?"

"Yes, as though I belong to the sea. I feel like the grain of sand here on the shore, a mere speck in the universe, and yet, it takes all of us specks to make the world revolve. We are part of the sea, part of the universe, part of each other."

He smiled down her. "Well said."

He drew in a deep breath that lifted his chest and pressed his side closer to hers. She placed a palm over his heart, feeling the strong thud of a warrior's heartbeat.

"What heavy thing is on your mind today, Prince Aleksandre?"

"Nothing heavy. The usual crises to thwart and decisions to be made."

"You're a good ruler, Aleks. Your countrymen adore you. When Antonia accompanied me into the city, tourists were spending money like crazy, the city is old-world gorgeous, and the Carvainian people seemed happy and thriving."

"True. The city thrives, but not all of Carvainia is this modern and prosperous. Last year floods wiped out hundreds of farms and villages. I took Nico there." She felt him tense. "I shouldn't have."

"Why do you say that? I'm sure he loved going with you."

"He did, but it was there he took ill. Something he contracted from the floodwaters destroyed his liver."

"Are you sure?"

"It was the only possible explanation."

"And you feel guilty, as though you were to blame."

"I was."

"You want to know something I'm learning about blame, Aleks?"

"What?"

"It has no value. It solves no problems."

He pondered for a bit before saying, "You've changed."

"Older, more wrinkles, fatter?" She tossed her head, hoping to make him smile. "Maybe some cellulite?"

The effort succeeded. Aleks laughed softly. "Older, yes, but also wiser—" his voice became tender as his fingers found the nape of her neck and massaged "—and infinitely more beautiful."

"Why, Mr. Prince, thank you. I'm flattered." Though her insides danced happily, Sara responded with a playful flutter of her eyelashes, refusing to let herself hope that his words were anything more than flattery from a smooth, cosmopolitan prince with a silver tongue.

But Aleks's expression had grown soft. His eyes caressed her face.

All the silliness fled. Sara swallowed, her tongue darting out to moisten dry lips. Aleks followed the action.

With the roar of the surf at his back and the wind whipping at her clothes, he groaned and slowly drew her closer. One hand in her hair, he tugged her head backward and pressed his lips to her throat. Sara shivered with sheer pleasure.

Aleks smiled against her skin. Then he worked his way to her waiting lips and kissed her with such tenderness she wanted to weep. How could a man claim to hate her and still kiss like that?

She wished the moment would never end but, of course, it did. Aleks grasped her hand and said, "Come. Let's walk awhile before the sun is up and the tourist boats come."

Sara cast an anxious glance toward the sea. "Tourists boats pass by here?"

"All day, every day, except in the family's private cove."

Feeling exposed and self-conscious, Sara wondered what a newspaper would give for a photo of their prince kissing a stranger on the seashore. A stranger in her robe.

"We shouldn't be together in plain sight like this. And you certainly shouldn't be kissing me. What if someone snaps a photo?"

He lifted one elegant shoulder. "I long ago stopped worrying about the press. Carvainians are generally protective of their royals."

"Tourists aren't polite Carvainians."

"Are you afraid to be photographed with me?"

"What a silly question. I would think it's the other way around. I'm the outsider. I no more fit here than a pig belongs in a ballet."

He chuckled. "I have something to ask you."

She glanced at the lightening sky and then at the still-empty water. "The sun is coming up. Ask quick."

"The crown is giving a Grand Ball this coming weekend."

"Yes, I know and I'll do my best to stay out of sight. Your mother mentioned it to me."

"She did? I find that interesting."

"Trust me, she wasn't inviting me to attend."

"She doesn't have to. I am."

She spun toward him so fast, her robe flared. "What?"

Aleks reached down, untied and retied the sash. After the bow was made, his hands lingered at her waist.

"*I* am hosting the affair. I would like you to attend as my guest."

Her belly was already going crazy from his touch, but now it leaped into her throat. Was she hearing correctly?

"But Duchess Philamena will be there."

Aleks loosened his hold on the belt to stare down at her, blinking, but he didn't step back. "Philamena? What do you know of the duchess?"

Apparently more than you would like. "Your mother believes Duchess Philamena is perfect for you."

"Perhaps. At least by Carvainian standards."

Her stomach dropped. "Your mother believes the two of you will marry."

He sighed and looked back toward the sky. "Yes, I know."

She waited, hoping he would assure her that no other woman held his heart. He didn't.

"Are you going to?" Please say no. Please say no.

He was silent for a moment, staring down at the white sand. When he answered, his voice was pensive. "I can't say."

It wasn't the answer she wanted to hear.

Sara turned, leaving Aleks alone as she ran up the incline and back into the castle.

# CHAPTER TEN

THE APRICOT ORCHIDS ARRIVED at midmorning, approximately an hour after she'd left Nico's playroom. The tender blossoms were accompanied by a vellum note embossed with the royal crest and seal. It said, "You will come to the Grand Ball. A."

Sara kept the orchids but turned the note over and wrote "No, I won't. S." and sent it back with a rather stunned-looking deliveryman.

A dressmaker arrived an hour later with sample gowns and a measuring tape. Sara thanked her kindly and tried to send her away. The woman wept.

"Ma'am, you are cruel. I cannot refuse the prince. Think what this will do to my reputation. I will lose my position as dressmaker to the royal family."

After a round of argument in which both Antonia and the dressmaker, Carlotta, insisted that Sara cooperate, if not for herself for the sake of the seamstress, Sara gave in.

"All right. You can make a dress, but I'm not wearing it."

The woman broke out in sobs again.

Horrified, Sara recanted. "Never mind. Stop crying. I will wear the dress." Under her breath she murmured, "But not to the Grand Ball."

She had no idea why Aleks wanted her to attend the function, but she was certain it was not for the reasons that mattered to her. Maybe he was being kind because of their shared past. Maybe he needed to discourage pursuing females. Whatever the reason, Sara couldn't go. The ball would only emphasize their differences and prove that a bookshop clerk from Kansas didn't belong with the Prince of Carvainia.

Long before Queen Irena had driven the point home, Sara had known she didn't fit in Aleks's world. She once had in America, but not here. Here, he would kiss her in a dark dungeon or under a dark sky where no one in the world could see. In the next breath, he'd admit that a wealthy duchess could one day be his bride. Sara accepted that he wanted her as he had in America.

This time, desire was not enough.

By afternoon when the women finally departed, Sara was anxious to see them go. She wanted to be with her son. Regardless of dresses or balls or kisses on the beach, her time in Carvainia grew short. A lifetime wasn't enough to spend with the child she'd given up at birth.

As she traversed the unusually empty corridor toward his rooms, she heard voices coming from inside an opened doorway.

"I want her released for travel immediately." The queen's precise, imperious command could not be mistaken.

Sara slowed, curious. The old adage that eavesdroppers never hear anything good about themselves came to mind. She started to hurry past, but Dr. Konstantine's words stopped her.

"I am a physician, my queen, not a magician. I cannot make her body heal before its time."

A prickle raised the hair on Sara's arms. They were discussing her!

"She and the prince are becoming close again. She must leave before she finds out the truth."

Sara's pulse began to drum erratically. What truth? What were they talking about?

She glanced down the hallways to be sure no one was watching. Then she edged closer to the door, staying out of sight.

"Perhaps the truth would serve us all better, my queen. The secret weighs heavily on you. Your blood pressure—"

A hiss of disgust from Irena. "Forget about my blood pressure. The crown is at stake. The secret must remain here in the castle and she must go before both of them discover what I did."

"All of your effort does not appear to have destroyed their feelings for one another."

"I did what I had to do for Prince Aleksandre and for all of Carvainia. The woman is a commoner, Doctor. A common American."

"Nonetheless, my queen, Prince Nico is her child."

At the mention of her son, Sara's heart pounded so hard, she feared the pair would hear it.

"The matter of Nico has been taken care of. Now you must do your part, Doctor. Get rid of Sara Presley." The queen's dismissive tone left no doubt that she'd issued an order and expected it to be followed.

At the sharp tap of heels against flooring, Sara jerked away from the door and made a dash for the stairwell. She pounded down the echoing steps to the next floor. A stitch pulled at her side. She stopped, breathless, panting, the ramifications of the overheard conversation swirling in her head.

What were they talking about? What had the queen done that she didn't want Sara and Aleks to find out about? And what did she mean that the matter of Nico had been taken care of? Was the venom in the queen's voice intended for Sara? Or for her son?

But queen Irena adored Nico. Didn't she?

Mind reeling, Sara stood with one hand on the closed stairwell door until she stopped shaking and normal breathing returned. The fear that something was terribly amiss refused to go away.

Aleks was teaching Nico the chess pieces when it happened.

"Papa, I don't want to play this." Nico rubbed the back of his hand over his eyes.

The boy was tired. His energy wasn't what it had been before the fateful trip to southern Carvainia. He was better, but far from his normal self. "Another time, then. The game will keep."

Aleks began gathering up the hand-carved chess pieces, rubbing his fingers over the smooth surface. The set had been in his family for generations. His own father had taught him to play with these very pieces. Just touching them made him feel close to his mentor, his idol, his beloved parent. Someday Nico would also appreciate this small, but meaningful connection with the line of monarchs who'd come before him.

"Papa."

"Hmm." Aleks carefully placed the kings into the velvet-lined case.

"Where is Sara?"

Aleks tensed, a bit surprised by the question. This was perhaps one of the few times in the day he hadn't been thinking about her. "I can't say. Why?"

"She didn't come. She always comes. I want her here."

Aleks understood the sentiment. As hard as he fought against feeling anything for her, Sara had burrowed beneath his skin. Perhaps Mother was right. It was time for him to find a wife.

"You haven't seen her today?" On the beach this morning

she'd become upset with something he'd said. He still didn't know what he'd done but he suspected his invitation to the Grand Ball had offended her somehow. A mystery, for certain. So he'd sent flowers and a dressmaker. "She can't be here every moment, son."

"Why?"

"Sara is a guest. Soon she will go back to America."

Nico's face crumpled. "Why can't she stay with us? Doesn't she like us? She said I was a good boy."

"I know for a fact that she likes you very much." Aleks tapped the tiny nose.

"She likes you, too, Papa."

He thought she did, but her affections could also be a ploy to gain custody of Nico. He didn't understand why she had changed her mind. She'd given the child away and now she wanted him back.

But he'd watched her with the boy. Her tears over the photo album had been real. It had taken him a long time, but he was starting to believe she truly loved their son.

And if she truly loved the son, what of the father? Could that have also been true?

"Perhaps she likes us both, my son, but Sara has a life in America. She wants to go home." Even as he spoke the words, he wondered if they were true. Sara's talk of her life in Kansas was factual but held little passion.

"I don't want her to go." Nico's bottom lip quivered.

"If we care about her, we can't be selfish. We'll want what's best for her."

His words mocked him. When had he wanted that? When had he ever considered what was best for Sara?

"Papa?"

"Yes?" By now, he'd lifted Nico onto his lap. The boy

curled into him, too-thin arms snaking around his neck. The balloon of joy that came only from Nico swelled inside Aleks.

"I love you."

"I love you, too."

"Is it okay if I love Sara a little bit, too?"

Aleks breathed in the sweet fragrance of his son's hair. "Love is magic. The more you give away, the more you have."

"Okay. I'll love her. She loves me. She told me when I was asleep. She kissed me, too." Nico touched his forehead. "Right there."

Aleks was at a loss for words, so he simply stroked Nico's straight, black hair and held him. For the first time, he considered the emotional toll this trip to Carvainia must be taking on Sara. He'd wanted her to suffer for abandoning their son, for abandoning him, too. And his wish had been granted.

He'd expected to feel triumph. He felt like a jerk.

Closing his eyes, he rested his cheek on Nico's head and tried not think so much about Sara Presley.

Nico's breathing grew slow and deep.

They both must have dozed for Aleks was suddenly jarred awake by his son's moans. Head fuzzy with images of Sara dancing through his dreams in a gauzy white gown, he felt the weight and heat of Nico against his chest. He tilted the child back into his arms.

"Nico, what's wrong?"

Nico looked at him with scared, glazed eyes. Then the terrible retching began.

Sara was taking a sundress from the armoire when the door to her suite suddenly banged open.

"Sara, hurry."

She spun around, arms instantly covering her state of undress, to find Aleks standing inside the room. He hadn't even knocked.

She started to protest, but one look at his face froze the words in her throat. Beneath the usual swarthy complexion, Aleks was pale as sand, and the stark terror in his eyes shot adrenaline into her veins.

All concern about being seen in her underwear evaporated. "What's wrong? It's Nico, isn't it?"

She knew even before his grim nod.

"He's taken ill again. Dr. Konstantine is deeply concerned."

"Oh, no."

Hands shaking, she grabbed the closest dress and dropped it over her head. Aleks crossed the room and raised the zipper while she shoved her feet into sandals.

"He asked for you." His breath brushed her neck.

"He did?" Had she not been so afraid, she would have rejoiced. But under the circumstances, her knees quaked.

"We've come so far. Nothing can go wrong now. He has to be all right."

Aleks extended a hand. It trembled. Stomach knotting, Sara grabbed on and they rushed out, anxious to be with their sick child.

When they reached the medical floor where Nico had been taken, the news was not good.

"My concern is for the health of the new liver," Dr. Konstantine said, his kind face particularly grave. "We've drawn blood to determine enzyme levels."

Sara had heard the terms enough during the last few weeks to understand. Elevated enzymes indicated possible damage to the liver. If Nico's transplanted organ failed, hope was gone. Her baby would die. She swallowed back a sob of agony. Histrionics would do no one any good.

"When will the results be known?" Aleks asked. The tension in his jaw was so tight, his lips barely moved. He was like a leashed tiger, ready to spring.

"I've ordered a rush on them but it will be hours at the least. Dr. Schlessinger is on his way from Switzerland now."

"What can he do that you haven't?"

"I can't say, Your Majesty, but he is the specialist."

"Is Nico awake? Can we go in?" Sara heard the fear and trembling in her voice.

"Of course." The doctor bowed slightly to Aleks. "I've given him a mild sedative to ease the sickness. He will sleep."

But Aleks was already tugging her through the doorway.

As too often had been the case, Prince Nico lay with eyes closed, looking fragile and ill. Thick black eyelashes brushed the crest of his cheeks. He was such a beautiful child.

A soft moan escaped Sara's lips. "I hate this."

Aleks said nothing, but he slid an arm around her waist and pulled her to his side. She was grateful, for she feared her legs would not hold her.

"What can we do?" she whispered.

"I wish I had the answer."

She tilted her head toward the ruler of Carvainia, a man in charge of an entire country, who was every bit as helpless as she.

"This is not your fault," she said. "Stop thinking about it."

She didn't know how she knew, but she did. Aleks would blame himself if the unthinkable occurred.

His gaze flicked down to hers and held. He swallowed, emotion emanating from him, though he kept himself in rigid check. "Thank you for that."

In that moment Sara realized a fascinating truth about Prince Aleksandre. He was a facade, the outward presentation of the real man she knew. As prince he had a duty to appear strong at all times. But the man inside hurt and struggled and felt just like everyone else. Only this man was alone in his pain.

Her heart reached out to him.

"Sometimes even a prince needs someone to lean on," she whispered, touching his granite-hard jaw. "You can lean on me, Aleks."

His eyes fell shut.

Sara wrapped both arms around his waist and rested her head against his chest. He engulfed her then, the trembling in his body matching hers.

They were like any other parents in the world, terrified for their dangerously ill child, and taking comfort in one another. In this space of time, they could forget their differences and focus on what really mattered—the health of their son.

And if the experience made her love them both even more, there was nothing at all she could do about it.

Three days crawled past in an agony of worry. Aleks canceled the Grand Ball and all but the absolute essential affairs of state. Neither he nor Sara slept much.

His mother was so upset she'd taken to her bed with another migraine. This worried Aleks, as well. The migraines had increased in frequency and intensity since Sara's arrival. Mother had begged him to send "that American" away so that they all might live in peace again. Though he agreed in theory, Aleks could not bring himself to force Sara to leave until Nico was stable.

He seriously wondered if he could send her away at all... But that was a problem he would deal with later. Nico was his focus now.

Doctors came and went. Tests were run and read. The young prince neither worsened nor improved, and the physicians began to suspect something other than host-graft issues. More tests were ordered until Nico whimpered in dread whenever a nurse or doctor entered the room.

Aleks wanted to command them to stop hurting his son. Sara must have felt the same for silent tears flowed down her cheeks as she and Aleks together held and comforted Nico during the blood draws.

She loved their son. Perhaps she hadn't when Nico was born, but she did now. In the endless nights and long days since Nico's latest crisis Sara slept little and ate less. If Nico moved, she was at his side instantly to caress and coo and tell him what a fine, brave boy he was.

At the moment, she slumped exhausted in a chair pulled close to Nico's side, one hand touching her child at all times. Her cinnamon hair lay lank and untended on her shoulders. Her eyes were red-rimmed and glassy. Yet, she refused to leave.

"You should sleep," he told her. "You have healing to do yourself. You can't heal if you don't rest."

"I'm all right." She shook her head. "I promised Nico I'd be here when he wakes so we can finish the gingerbread story. You go. You have a country to run and you're so tired you can barely stand."

She was not far from right. During the two-year war with Perseidia, he had faced fatigue and despair, but nothing like this. This was his son.

He scrubbed both hands down his face. "No. I cannot leave. What if he—?"

Aleks could not voice the terrible fear. What if his son, his only beloved child, died? They'd had such hope in the days following the transplant. And now, this.

Sara reached out and squeezed his hand without comment. She understood, and the bond between them deepened.

The door whispered open and Dr. Schlessinger, a white lab coat covering his gray suit, entered the room. Both adults swiveled toward the specialist.

"Doctor?" The tension in the room was thicker than London fog.

"Miss Presley." The doctor nodded toward Sara and then spoke to Aleksandre. "Sir, may I have a word with you in the hallway?"

Aleks glanced at Sara and saw the hope and worry etched in her face. "You may speak in front of Miss Presley."

The specialist bowed slightly. "As you wish. In our search for answers, I ordered a number of tests to rule out every possible, even improbable, cause. I did not expect to find anything."

"But you did?"

"Unfortunately."

Aleks gut tightened. "Meaning?"

By this time, Sara had risen and moved to Aleks's side. Without giving the action any thought, he reached down and clasped her cold fingers. She held tight, a small but comforting anchor in a great storm.

"One of the tests revealed a disturbing drug in Nico's system."

"He's been given many drugs since his illness began."

"Indeed. But no knowledgeable person would administer acetaminophen to a child with liver disease."

"I'm afraid I don't understand, Doctor. Explain please."

Dr. Schlessinger adjusted his wire-rim glasses. "Acetaminophen is a common and generally safe analgesic, but it is stressful to the liver, especially to a liver already struggling to function. In large doses the drug can cause liver failure, even death."

Aleks blinked, not confused exactly but wary. "Then why was it ordered? Who gave it?"

"That is the most bewildering issue, Your Majesty. There is no order on his charts and no record that Nico has ever taken the medication. But it is undeniably in his system."

Sara's sharp intake of breath sounded loud in the quiet room. "Someone gave it to him secretly? Why? Are you saying someone tried to hurt him?"

"We would hope not, madam. Our thoughts are otherwise. Dr. Konstantine assures me that the child is quite safe here. He is much beloved by all." He gave her a small, bloodless smile. "We conclude, therefore, that someone thought they were helping the little prince. When he complained of discomfort some kindhearted though misguided soul gave him acetaminophen believing it harmless."

"When, in fact," Aleks growled, teeth tight with the implications, "the drug is killing him."

"Exactly."

"But who would give Nico medication without discussing it with Dr. Konstantine?" The very idea infuriated him. "Everyone in the palace knows of his delicate condition."

"You will have to discuss that with your staff."

"You can be assured I will."

Aleks clenched his fists. Anger bubbled up like hot lava. Sara squeezed his arm reassuringly, but he was not to be mollified. Someone within the palace was responsible for Nico's condition. Even if accidental, there was no acceptable excuse.

"Now that we suspect the cause, we have an antidote," the doctor continued. "The nurse is preparing it as we speak."

"Thank God." Sara's body sagged against Aleks. Somehow his arms had circled her waist, and his hand now rode on her hip bone. He gave a gentle squeeze, trying to reassure her. "Will this make him well?"

"Time will tell. Hopefully, we have caught the problem

before irreparable damage is done to the new organ." The doctor started to leave, then stopped and turned around, pale blue eyes piercing in their intensity. "But you must inform everyone who comes in contact with the boy that he is never to have acetaminophen again. Ever."

"You need not concern yourself about that, Doctor," Aleks said. "I will deliver the message loud and clear."

"Very good." The doctor dipped his head. "Good night then."

"Good night. And thank you."

After Dr. Schlessinger departed Aleks's shoulders relaxed, though his mind buzzed with the news. Nico would recover but someone had made a deadly mistake. And that someone must be found before the mistake was repeated.

He moved to Nico's bed and gazed down at the beloved boy. "I am relieved to have a solution but also upset that such a serious error could occur. Why would anyone give medication to a seriously ill child without consulting the physician in charge?"

Sara had come to stand next to him. Oddly, he was still holding her hand and until this second, had not realized it.

"I don't know," she said, "but the possibilities scare me."

Aleks recalled her earlier insistence that someone wished Nico intentional harm. He still didn't believe it. He couldn't. Not someone in his own household.

"You don't think the acetaminophen was an accident, do you?" he asked quietly, gazing down at the gleam of red hair over her temple.

"No, I don't. Not for one minute." She cast a pensive look at the sleeping face of their son before capturing Aleks's gaze with hers. She reached for his other hand, holding both in her chilled grip. "And you may hate me all over again when I tell you what else I think."

# CHAPTER ELEVEN

SARA SHOOK FROM THE TOP of her head to the bottom of her feet. The coming confrontation was not something she relished, but for her baby's sake, she would face the devil himself.

Last night, Nico had rallied after the administration of the antidote and subsequent medications to cleanse his new liver. It was clear now that acetaminophen, a common pain reliever, had caused Nico's bouts of illness. What wasn't clear was who gave him the drug.

Sara didn't know, but she had some ideas, and she would never believe the overdose was accidental. Someone wanted to hurt her baby. The questions were who and why?

Long after midnight, she had fallen into an exhausted, dreamless slumber. Antonia had awakened her moments ago to the smell of French roast coffee and waffles swimming in butter and maple syrup.

"His Majesty said these were your favorites."

"He remembered that?" Sara fought back a blush, realizing she'd said too much. Antonia did not know of her and Aleks's former relationship. She might suspect but she'd not been informed.

To cover up, Sara said, "I mentioned it to him the other day, but I never expected him to remember. I mean, he's a prince and all with so much on his mind."

Antonia only smiled and Sara worried that she'd babbled on too long.

Now that breakfast was over and she'd soaked away some of her fatigue and stress in a fragrant jetted tub, Sara could procrastinate no more.

Last night, Aleks had refused to discuss her suspicions. He'd called her overwrought and too tired to think clearly. He'd been right on that account, but this morning after rest and food, she was more determined than ever to find out who might intentionally want to harm her son.

Her first concern was the smiling nurse, Maria, but the woman had never actually done anything suspicious. She'd simply been present before several of Nico's bouts of illness. Even though she gave Sara an odd feeling, that was not enough to accuse her of attempted murder. Maria was the grieving mother of a fallen hero. She'd given her all to the service of the royal family. Aleks thought highly of her.

Sara blew out a discouraged breath. Maybe she had been wrong about Maria.

Then who?

Aleks admitted having enemies, particularly the King of Perseidia. Would the king have sent a spy into Castle-by-the-Sea to murder Prince Aleksandre's son? Why Nico instead of Aleks? Revenge of the most heinous kind?

Or what if the perpetrator was a radical Carvainian? Every country had them, those who wanted a perfect society. What if that person knew Nico was not full-blood Carvainian?

No, that was unlikely. Though rumors had raced like Thoroughbreds since Sara's arrival, very few people in the castle had that information. To the nation at large, Nico was their little crown prince, a Carvainian through and through.

Reluctantly, her thoughts turned to Queen Irena. The queen knew of Nico's parentage, and she loathed the "common American" who had given him life. At the same time, she appeared to adore Nico. She was his grandmother. Surely not the queen.

And yet, who else knew except Dr. Konstantine? Would the gentle doctor do such a thing to a child?

Both of them had been discussing Sara and Nico in a less than friendly manner.

With a sigh, Sara drained the rest of her coffee and plunked the cup onto the saucer. Her head ached with trying to figure it out.

Even if she knew who to blame, she could do nothing until she spoke to Aleks. He *had* to listen to her. She must convince him of the danger before the enemy, whoever it might be, tried something more desperate.

At the thought of discussing her concerns with Aleks, dread weighed her down. The light, tender waffles lay like bricks in her stomach. These were his people. People he trusted. People he loved. How could she ever convince him that one of them was evil? He would think her either mad or a troublemaker.

In the three days of agonizing over Nico, she and Aleks had supported and comforted one another. They'd grown closer, talking in quiet whispers during those endless hours from midnight until dawn. He'd been Aleks as she knew him. Not a warrior. Not a prince. Just a scared father.

Often during the long days and nights they'd sat without talking, hands clasped in silent support. When she'd dozed, she'd awakened to find Aleks covering her with a velvet-soft blanket. When she'd blinked up at him, he'd smiled tiredly, kissed her forehead, and said, "Sleep. I'll wake you if anything happens."

She'd believed him.

If he ever slept during those long nights and days, she hadn't seen it.

She'd even begun to think he might soften his stance on allowing her contact with Nico in the future. Worse still, she'd started to believe he cared for her.

After this morning, he'd hate her all over again.

The red uniformed butler with the stiffest back in the world gestured her into Aleks's office. She'd phoned the prince's private number, expressed her desire to talk, and he'd invited her here. She'd expected him to be resting but he was back at work, as though he'd slept for days.

As soon as he saw her, he tossed aside his pen and rose to embrace her.

She leaned into him, relishing the moment. After this conversation, he might never touch her again. She breathed him in, absorbing all the nuances of Aleks. Subtle, expensive cologne. Powerful, leashed muscles wrapped in a perfectly tailored suit.

Saints above, she loved him.

"I can't believe you're working," she said when she stepped back a little. "You look like death warmed over."

Still holding her upper arms, the corners of his mouth tilted. "Flattery, my darling?"

His darling. An impossible dream.

Sara touched his smooth-shaved jaw. "Will you rest? You have to rest. He's going to be all right now."

His chest heaved. "I could not have borne these last days without you."

"I'm glad I could be here. Thank you for giving me that much."

"No gratitude is required. You are his mother."

Sara's eyes filled with tears. She'd waited a long time to hear those words. "Oh, Aleks. This is so hard."

He kissed her temple. "Hard? What is hard? Being Nico's mother?"

She shook her head. "No. Never that. It's all I ever wanted." Well, not all. She'd wanted to be Aleks's wife, as well, but she couldn't tell him her impossible dream.

He cocked his head, dark, dark eyes searching her face. "Then what? You have a sadness about you this morning."

She broke away and went to the window overlooking the seashore. The day was overcast, an unusual occurrence. Waves crashed against the sand, harbingers of a coming storm.

Sara wondered if the storm outside would be repeated inside this office.

"There's something I have to discuss with you, Aleks. Even if it makes you angry, you must consider what I have to say."

She heard the soft pad of his footsteps across the plush carpeting as he came to her side. "The sea is wild today."

"I was thinking the same thing."

"Were you?"

"Partly." Her head swiveled in his direction. Standing ramrod straight, he looked as powerful and dangerous as the sea, and every bit as magnificent. "Aleks?"

"Speak. I can tell you have something heavy on your mind."

"You aren't going to like it."

"Is this about Prince Nico?"

"Yes."

"I've been giving the situation some thought."

"So you agree that the overdose was not accidental?"

He gave her a strange look. "The overdose?"

"Yes. Wasn't that what you meant?"

"No." But he didn't elaborate, and Sara was left to wonder what "situation" he'd been considering. Instead, he said, "Dr. Konstantine agrees that someone likely gave Nico the medicine in ignorance."

She knew he didn't want to hear it, but she had to say, "What if they didn't, Aleks? What if it was intentional?"

"It was not."

Pigheaded Carvainian. "Are you willing to bet your son's life on it?"

He laced his hands behind his neck and stared up at the ceiling. "You are determined to fight about this."

"I am determined to protect my son."

"And you think I am not?"

"No! You adore Nico. You would do anything to protect him."

"Correct. If it soothes you to know, I have taken every precaution. Security is alerted to your concerns. A camera has been placed inside Nico's room. An extra guard keeps watch."

There was a measure of comfort in knowing that he hadn't completely ignored her. "But what if Nico is in danger from someone the guards trust?"

"Maria again? Will you continue to malign my best friend's mother?"

"I'm sorry. I know you hate that, but we have to consider her and anyone else with easy access to Nico's rooms."

"Certainly, but the question is why? Why would anyone within these walls want to harm the crown prince?"

"Maybe for precisely that reason. Because he *is* the crown prince."

Something in his tight demeanor changed. Sara could see the wheels turning inside his brilliant head. "Elaborate, please."

Taking a deep, shaky breath, Sara started with the idea of a radical Carvainian. Aleks's eyes narrowed and he nodded. "Possible. But who?"

"I don't know. It could be anyone, but I've wondered about Dr. Konstantine as well as Maria. They are often with Nico."

A muscle twitched below his right eye. "Are you determined to make me angry this morning?"

She shook her head. "No. I only want to keep Nico safe." She grasped Aleks's hand and brought it to her cheek. "The last thing I want is to make you angry."

"Then don't." He moved closer, turning his hand to brush the knuckles over her cheek. "Let us celebrate our son's recovery."

"But—" He placed a finger over her lips.

"Shh. Today I have hope. Don't take it from me."

Torn between what she feared and what she yearned for, Sara's heart sank lower and lower. He would hate her once she mentioned the queen.

He drew her close and she went to him, belly fluttering with conflicting desires. Soon she would destroy this sweet emotion brewing between them, so for these precious moments, she would let him hold her. And she would pretend he loved her enough.

His warm, supple mouth found hers, and she was lost in him for a few, wonderful seconds. When he lifted his head to gaze tenderly at her, her pulse rattled wildly against her collarbone. She saw something in his eyes, a look she'd seen before, years ago. A look she'd never expected to see again. Hope and despair mingled like warring sisters.

"Aleks," she whispered.

"You are like a drug in my blood, Sara Presley. The more I have of you, the more I want. And yet—"

It was her turn to place a finger to his lips. "Shh."

She wasn't ready to remember the reasons they could never be. She knew them better than he did. Right now, she wanted to love him and be with him in this sweet moment when Nico was healing and they were at peace. Soon enough, the storm would break and she would be washed away in a sea of his anger.

"Remember," she said, caressing his face, tracing his lips and noble jaw, "the first time I cooked for you?"

"I remember everything about our time together."

"You do?"

The corners of his eyes crinkled. "The casserole was hideous and you cried."

"And you ate it anyway."

His face softened. "Because I loved you."

"Yes. And I loved you, Aleks. Then and now. Nothing has changed my feelings."

He inhaled deeply and drew her against his chest, saying nothing. His heart thudded beneath her ear.

"It's okay, Aleks. I understand." He was a royal and she wasn't. They were from different worlds and different backgrounds. The only things they had in common were love for their son and a passion for each other.

"I don't think you do," he murmured against her hair. "If you loved me, why did you give away our child?"

His voice was weary, as though he'd struggled with the question for a long time. "I've explained what happened. I hate what I did, but I thought you'd abandoned me."

"You see, Sara, this is where the story becomes a problem. I did not abandon you. I sent someone to you."

"Who?"

"My mother, and she returned with the news that you wanted nothing to do with me or with my child."

"That's not true." The knot in Sara's stomach twisted until her belly ached. "I don't care what you were told. That is not true."

Aleks stiffened. All the tenderness they'd been sharing disappeared. "My mother would not lie."

She'd opened this can of worms. As much as she dreaded the end result, she couldn't stop now until everything was said.

"But what if she did? She despises me, Aleks. I'm an American commoner. What if she lied to get me out of your life?"

He jerked away from her. "I will not hear this."

"Yes, you will." She reached for him, imploring. "You're going to hate me anyway, so I have to tell you everything. I overheard your mother and Dr. Konstantine talking. Your mother wants to get rid of me. I heard her say so. I also heard her say, 'the problem of Nico has been resolved.' What does that mean, Aleks? What problem of Nico has she resolved? Is my son a problem because he's half-American and not worthy to take the throne?"

Aleks went as still as death. Disbelief rose from his stiffened body like heat from a tin roof.

When he spoke, his tone was low and threatening. "Are you accusing the queen of trying to murder her own grandson?"

"No." Sara shoved at a lock of hair, frustrated, distraught, and terrified that she was making a huge mistake. But Nico's life was at stake. She had to bring every possibility into the light. "Aleks, I don't know. Maybe I'm wrong—"

"You most decidedly are."

"But what if I'm not? You have to consider the possibility."

"Enough." Face dark and livid, he chopped the air with his hand.

Sara latched onto his forearm with both hands. "No. You will listen to me, you pigheaded prince. Someone lied to you, and it wasn't me. Someone kept me away from my baby—and the man I loved—for five years. And now, someone has poisoned Nico. We don't know why, but you have to consider that there are people who are not pleased at having a future prince who is not purely Carvainian. You have to consider everything."

He shook her off as if she were lint on his suit. "Your accusations are ridiculous."

"What if they aren't? What if I'm right?"

"You are accusing the one person in this world who I trust with my life. She is my mother and she is a good and beloved queen. If not for her, I would never have known my son." He whirled away to storm across the room. Outside the rain cried against the windows.

Sara followed him, intent on making him understand. As she'd feared, her suspicions had destroyed the sweet relationship developing between them. There was no point in stopping now until Aleks agreed to investigate every potential reason for Nico's illness.

She knew for certain that Queen Irena had developed an elaborate plot five years ago. Could she still be plotting?

"If not for the queen, I would never have been forced to give Nico up for adoption in the first place. We could have been together."

"You don't know what you're talking about." Aleks turned, eyes hard, though the emotion behind them was raging. "I was warned that bringing you here would cause trouble, but I was determined to save Nico's life at all costs."

"That's what I care about, too, Aleks. Please believe me. I'm not trying to cause a problem. I just want my son to be safe."

"From his own grandmother? Woman you are insane, a pathetic, ranting lunatic. My mother was right. You are a dangerous woman."

"Listen to me, Aleks, please. I'm only asking you to check into everyone and everything. I'm not trying to accuse her or anyone. I'm just scared and confused and—"

"And finished."

Sara went as still as the tomb. "What?"

He stalked to his desk and yanked open a drawer. "We have a contract. It is completed."

Sara rocked back. "I don't understand."

"Your vacation in Carvainia is over. Your visa is hereby revoked. I will alert the staff to prepare for your departure."

Sara's hand went to her throat. "Aleks, no. Please. I can't leave my son."

"He is not yours."

"I beg you not to do this. Give me a little more time. Please."

He thrust an envelope toward her. "Here is what you came for, the one thing I know that matters to you. Take it and go."

She drew back. "No."

He pried her clenched fingers open and forced the envelope into her grasp. "I do not wish to see your face again. Goodbye, Sara Presley."

And with that, he spun on the heel of his gleaming shoes and stormed out.

Sara couldn't move. She couldn't breathe. In fact, she didn't want to. She wanted her rampaging heart to cease beating so she could die right here in Aleks's office.

The room grew cold and her knees trembled. Outside the storm had broken upon a swirling, surging sea.

The storm had broken inside the castle, as well.

She glanced down at the envelope in her shaking hand. Slowly, she opened it to find the dreaded contract. She'd agreed to give Nico life in exchange for one million dollars.

The bank draft was like a snake in her hand. She hated it. Why had she ever agreed to such a travesty?

She tore the draft into small pieces and replaced it in the envelope. With feet of lead, she walked to the desk.

"All I ever wanted was you, Aleks. You and our son." She opened the top drawer and slid the envelope inside.

But not before the paper was wet with tears.

# CHAPTER TWELVE

"Saddle Windstar."

"Sir. Your Majesty, begging your pardon, but you should not go out in this storm."

Aleks speared the groom with a look. "Saddle him."

"As you wish."

In moments, Aleks was astride the sleek black horse and galloping headlong across the castle grounds. The cold rain slashed against his face, but he barely felt it. He needed to ride and to think. If only his father were still alive, they would ride together and laugh at the storm. They would solve the problems of the nation and of the heart.

But his father was gone.

The curse of being a ruling prince was the terrible aloneness. Though surrounded by people much of the time, there was no one to whom he could turn, no one with whom to share his heartache, no one to offer comfort or wisdom.

Without warning, his thoughts went to these last three days and nights at Nico's bedside. Sara had been there for him. She had felt his pain. She'd been his comfort and strength and shared his burden.

But now she accused his mother of lying and perhaps even of attempted murder?

The rage of such a ludicrous accusation had passed and he simply felt bereft. Sara had fooled him again. He'd started to believe that they could set things right somehow.

The queen had been right all along. Sara had her own agenda. She'd done nothing but stir up trouble since she'd entered the castle. Nico would be brokenhearted to know his new friend was abandoning him—again.

Aleksandre should have never allowed the contact with his son to begin with, but Sara had outmaneuvered him.

He dug his heels into Windstar and felt the spurt of power beneath him. Windstar would run until his lungs exploded, though he was not overly fond of storms. When lightning shimmered in the distance and thunder rumbled the horse reared slightly. Aleks held strong, bringing him down. The animal pranced sideways, head shaking. Aleks patted the quivering neck. "Easy, old man."

They were a matched pair, the horse and the prince. The horse instinctively seemed to understand the prince's need to let the wind and the rain and the ride purge his tattered mind. Both horse and man were soaked through, and yet they thundered on. Past the dozens of outbuildings, past the private cove and down to the sea. Waves crashed over the sand and sent sea spray up the beach for more than a hundred yards. Aleks pulled up, he and the horse facing the endless expanse of dark, boiling sea and sky.

He saw her there as they'd been that one morning when she came to him in white robe and bare feet. She'd brought with her something he'd never expected to experience again. She'd brought love. At least, he'd thought as much.

On that twilight morning with the moon white above and air warm and redolent of the seagull's song, she'd broken down his rigidly erected wall. He'd built a fortress against her and she'd walked through it on bare feet.

A man's heart was a traitorous thing.

He'd started to believe her assertions that Nico was in danger. He was not a fool. The possibility was real. But not from Nico's own grandmother.

A vivid flash of lightning danced over the waves. He held tight to Windstar's reins and the big gelding didn't falter this time.

Aleks had no doubt about his mother's negative feelings toward Sara. Sara was bright. She felt the hostility.

Perhaps Sara was trying to cause dissension between him and his mother because the queen was wise to her ways.

Yet, as hard as he tried to envision Sara as the villain, his heart bled with wanting her.

But the die was cast. She must leave before he became more of a fool than he'd already been.

He turned the big steed up the coast, letting the driving rain pound into his face, and rode them both into exhaustion.

"I'm coming home tomorrow." Sara heard the quiver in her voice as she talked to Penny.

"What's wrong? You sound upset."

"Aleks asked me to leave." She lay prostrate on the massive canopy bed, clothes strewn around her. She didn't want to go. Not yet. Not ever.

"Prince Jerk. I don't know what you ever saw in him."

He wasn't always a jerk. Sometimes he was warm and funny and loving. "He adores our son."

"Did he agree to visitation?"

Sara rubbed a hand down her throat. Antonia had lit a scented candle but the smell set her stomach to churning. She was sick, all right. Sick with grief. "No."

A beat of silence. "What are you going to do?"

"I don't know yet. Right now, I'm coming home. Maybe

I can figure out something later. At least I know where my baby is now."

"And you know he's safe. Remember how you used to worry about that?"

Sara's eyes fell shut. She still worried about his safety, but she didn't say as much to Penny. "I need to hang up now, Penny. I want to spend as much time with Nico as I can before tomorrow."

She glanced at the clock. If only she could stop time.

"Okay." And then, "Sara, I'm sorry. I never should have made you go on that fake vacation."

"Don't apologize, Penny. As sad as I am tonight, it was the best thing that has happened to me in years."

That much was true. Though she had no idea how she would get through the days ahead, this time with Nico and Aleks was worth any amount of suffering.

After they ended the call, Sara looked at her meager belongings but didn't pack. Antonia had insisted the job be left for her. Fine. She didn't want to pack anyway. She wanted to run and lock herself in the dungeon where no one could find her, sneaking out at night to see her son.

Shaking her head at the ludicrous fantasy, she went to the closet for a sweater to wear against the cool air brought on by the storm. The ball gown hung there, a vision of aquamarine satin. It was the most beautiful garment Sara had ever owned. She let her fingers drift over the smooth fabric before closing the closet and heading to Nico's room.

A rumble of thunder drew her to the window. The storm had not let up for nearly an hour.

Sweater over her shoulders, she stared out at the sluicing rain. In the distance, a lone figure rode a dark horse with as much wildness as the storm.

Her heart lurched.

"Aleks." She placed the palm of her hand against the cold windowpane as though she could touch him.

He looked as alone as she felt. No, more so. Aleks carried the weight of his family, his people, his nation on his shoulders. And he carried it well. He was an excellent leader. His people loved him.

So did she.

Fool that she was. Her heart still reached out for him.

As the thought came, he rode out of sight, as lost to her as if they'd never been.

Sara spent the late afternoon and evening playing with her son. The attendants, accustomed to her presence, went about their business and for the most part left her and Nico alone. Though she wondered if someone would come along and force her to leave at Aleks's orders, no one did.

Regardless of her false smile, Sara's heart was heavy and a thick knot of dread had settled in her stomach. This evening would fly by. Tomorrow she would be gone from her beloved child and his equally beloved father. Perhaps she'd never see either of them again, a painful possibility she wasn't ready to face.

She puffed gently against the bubble wand. An iridescent soap bubble emerged and hung suspended above Nico's enchanted face.

He clapped his hands. "I see a rainbow."

Sara laughed, storing the memories of every moment. "Now you blow one."

With great concentration, Nico dipped the circular wand into the bubble jar and blew. His eyes widened with amazement as the bubble grew larger and larger before popping. He jerked back. "It splashed me."

Sara laughed again and Nico joined her. She grabbed her cell phone and videotaped the sight and sound of his laughter.

"Let me see." Nico leaned in toward the small screen. The little boy smell of playtime and Play-Doh was a scent Sara would never forget.

"You're a handsome boy."

"You are, too." And then he giggled. "You're not a boy."

She rubbed her nose against his. "No. I'm a...silly rabbit."

His nose wrinkled with glee. "You are not. You're a girl. A real pretty girl. I like your hair, too." His little hands stroked the side of her head. Sara closed her eyes from the pure joy of being caressed by her son.

Would he remember these moments? Would he ever know that the woman who sang silly songs and blew bubbles and finger-painted the sea and the sun was his mother?

Would she ever see him again?

As the evening slipped away, Sara struggled with how to break the news of her departure. She had to tell him, for her sake as well as his.

Finally, when they were in the midst of a jigsaw puzzle, she said, "I have something important to tell you, Nico."

His intelligent face tilted upward with happy expectation. "A surprise?"

"No, not really a surprise." Determined to keep the departure light, she smiled, though the action felt as fake as this "vacation." "I will be going back to America tomorrow. We may not see each other again before my plane leaves. And I want you to know that meeting you has been the best thing in my whole life. You are a wonderful boy."

His face fell. His fingers tightened on a piece of puzzle.

"But I don't want you to go, Miss Sara. I want you to stay here and play with me."

"My vacation time is over, Nico. I'm sorry." So sorry that her stomach hurt and her heart was shattering in her chest. "Staying would be lovely, but I'm afraid I cannot."

"Papa said you're lonely for America."

"He did, did he?" So Aleks had already been preparing the boy for her to leave. He must have intended all along to find a reason to rid the country of her, and she'd made the task so easy.

"When will you return? In one week? Papa always promises to return in one week." His handsome face twisted. "Or sometimes two when he goes far, far away. Will you come again in two weeks?"

Sara forced her breathing to appear normal, though tears burned her throat. "No, darling boy, not in two weeks."

"When?"

Staring down at a yellow puzzle piece to hide her tears, she said, "I don't know, sweetheart. I just don't know. America is very far away."

Nico pressed a piece into place before raising puzzled eyes to hers. "But you will come back, won't you?"

Not knowing what else to say, Sara said, "If I can, I will come again."

The answer was enough for the four-year-old. He picked up a green-and-brown puzzle piece, examined it, and snapped it into place. A dinosaur was beginning to emerge.

"Papa says you have a bookstore in America."

So he and Aleks had discussed her. She wondered why. "Yes, I do, with lots and lots of books exactly right for little boys."

"Books about horses?"

"Lots of books about horses." She thought of Aleks riding like the wind along the seashore. "Perhaps I can send you one."

"I have a pony. When I am well Papa will allow me to ride again."

Sara longed to see that day. She longed for the time when Nico was well enough to run and play like a normal boy. But regardless of his return to health, Nico d'Gabriel would never be a normal boy. Like his father, he was bound by the rules and conventions of his inherited place in Carvainian society. And like his father, he would someday be a fine ruler. Even though she would not be here to watch him grow, she had no doubt Aleks would raise him to become a fine man.

As long as he was kept safe.

Her gut tightened at the thought that would not go away. What if Aleks and the doctors were wrong? What if Nico remained in danger and she was the only one who suspected? How could she leave when he was still vulnerable and when the person who'd overdosed him had still not been discovered?

Aleks was certain palace security could adequately protect their son if needed, but the guards had not stopped someone from poisoning his new liver with acetaminophen. What if the old liver had been intentionally destroyed in the same way? What if Nico had not contracted a viral illness during the flood zone trip as suspected?

The notion shot a spear of terror through her soul.

With all her might, she prayed that the doctors were right and the overdose was nothing more than an unfortunate accident. Maybe she was simply too overwrought and overprotective. Perhaps the stress of these strange weeks had distorted her thinking.

She wished she could believe that.

"May I come to your bookstore sometime, Sara?"

Unwilling and unable to admit that Aleks would never allow such a thing, Sara gathered the thin body into her arms.

"I would love for you to visit my bookstore. You can choose any book you want."

"When I am well Papa will bring me." The phrase had become a mantra to Nico. When he was well again he wanted to do so many things.

"Don't be sad if he doesn't. America is a long way to travel."

"Papa has an airplane. He likes you, too. He will come."

The words brought a renewed ache to her heart. She'd begun to believe Aleks cared for her, as well. She'd even dreamed he could love her again, but a dream was all it was or could ever have been. She hadn't known that in America. Now, she did.

But even though Aleks was a ruling prince destined to marry a duchess or a princess, Sara would always be the mother of this child. Not even Irena could change that.

She rested a hand atop her son's head. "If Papa will bring you, you can come to visit me in America anytime. I will be waiting."

*For the rest of my life.*

The rest of the evening passed far too quickly as they played and talked, sang songs and made up rhymes. Too soon, the nanny reappeared.

"It is time for Prince Nico's bath." The woman held a hand out. Nico's little shoulders drooped in resignation.

"I could give him his bath," Sara offered, almost too eagerly. Every moment grew more precious as the clock ticked cruelly forward.

The nanny seemed taken aback by the suggestion. "But this is my duty. You are a guest."

"Please. I'm leaving tomorrow." She kept the tone light, lest she break down in front of her son. "Tonight is my last night in Carvainia. I'd like to spend as much time with Prince Nico as possible."

The woman studied her with dark Carvainian eyes and Sara wondered if she suspected that there was more to the relationship between Sara and Nico than a donor and recipient. "His Highness will miss you, ma'am. And all of Carvainia will be forever grateful for your sacrifice."

"It was no sacrifice," she said honestly. "Nico has won my heart."

The nanny tweaked Nico's chin with a smile. "He has that effect upon everyone."

Sara hoped that was true, but the warning bell inside her mother's head would not shut off.

"That bath?" she asked.

The nanny's face softened. "Certainly, if Prince Nico agrees."

The boy was already selecting toys to take into the water. "I want Sara to see my boat. It's blue like Papa's. And it goes, *brrr, brrr, brrr* in the water." His little mouth made a motorboat noise that had the women sharing indulgent smiles.

Keeping her plastic smile in place, Sara went to give her son a bath for the first time…as well as the last.

Long after, when Nico was freshly scrubbed and smelling of bubble-gum-scented soap, Sara dressed him in pajamas and tucked him into his own bed. Now that the acute illness was over, he'd been returned to the normal nursery suite in the family wing.

Knowing that Aleks's room was only steps away gave Sara a strange feeling. She wanted to see him, but she didn't. Sad to say, she feared he'd drive her out of Nico's room. Tonight she would fight to stay.

But the thought of leaving Carvainia without one more

glimpse of him and without a final chance to set things right, hurt almost more than she could stand.

"One more story, Sara?" Nico's eyes fluttered shut but he forced them open again. "One more."

She'd read until her throat was sore and the nanny had retired for the night. Still, she was as reluctant as her son to end the evening.

"One more." She selected a board book and began to read the gentle rhyming text about a little train that would not give up. Nico wanted to see the colorful pictures but by book's end, he could stay awake no longer. His eyes fell shut, the thick black lashes fluttering against his cheeks like dark butterflies. Clad in race car pajamas, his thin chest rose and fell in peaceful slumber.

Sara closed the book and held it in her lap, gazing down at her son with all the love bottled up inside. After the longest time, she snapped off the lamp, leaving only the sailboat night-light to cast a glow in the room. She leaned forward and kissed him.

"I love you, Nico," she whispered against his velvet cheek. "Your mommy will always love you."

The night had come too soon. She was not yet ready to be separated from her heart and soul. So she remained on the edge of the mattress, watching her baby sleep. Tomorrow night, she'd have only the memories.

When the night deepened, Sara began to nod, too tired and emotionally spent to remain upright. Unwilling to leave her son's side on this final time in his company, she lay down on a rug between the bed and wall. No one would see her here. No one would ask her to leave. Not even Aleks.

Sara stretched one hand onto the bed to touch Nico and then she dozed.

She didn't know how long she slept, but some time later, Sara awakened with a start. Suddenly alert, she remained still, listening. Had she heard a noise? She listened hard, barely breathing.

Nothing except the rhythmic in and out of her son's breathing.

It occurred to her then that she was no longer touching Nico's foot. With a self-deprecating huff, she pulled her sweater closer against the chill. The noise she'd heard must have been her own hand falling off the bed.

But then the noise came again. An infinitesimal squeak of movement.

Her pulse kicked up. Someone *was* in the room. And that someone moved slowly across the floor and came to a stop on the other side of Nico's bed.

Swallowing a lump of anxiety, Sara eased up to her knees.

What she saw made her blood run cold. A woman, shadowed by darkness, stood over Nico with a syringe in hand.

Sara leaped to her feet and demanded, "What are you doing?"

The woman jerked back, eyes blinking rapidly in confusion. In the night-light a familiar, ghostly face stared across at Sara.

"Maria," she whispered. Her suspicions about the usually smiling nurse pushed to the front.

"It's time for his medication." There was something hard and desperate in the other woman's voice.

A shot of fear-fueled adrenaline surged through Sara. Something was very wrong.

"He's not supposed to have anything else tonight." She stretched across the bed to grasp Maria's upraised wrist. "What are you giving him?"

And why are you doing it under cover of darkness?

Maria yanked. Sara held fast.

A tug of war ensued. Leaning across the wide bed, Sara was in an awkward position, but she was not about to give in.

"He must have it. He must." Maria's eyes widened to a point of wildness. Tension corded the veins in her neck. "You don't understand."

"Then let's call Dr. Konstantine. He can explain."

"No!" she shouted. "Time is running out, you stupid American. All you've done is cause problems. It would have been over if not for you."

Fear grew with every word that tumbled from the nurse's mouth. "What would be over?"

"Recompense. Carlo deserves recompense."

Sara clung hard to Maria's hand. One slip and she could plunge the poison into Nico's vulnerable body.

"It was you, wasn't it? It was you trying to hurt Nico." As she spoke, Sara held tight to the nurse's wrist and crawled across the bed to form a shield between Maria and the child.

With a hiss, Maria yanked hard. Unbalanced, Sara lost her grip and fell headlong onto the floor. She watched in horror as the syringe plunged through the thigh of Nico's pajamas. The child awoke with a scream. His small hands instinctively pushed at the offending needle.

Terrified, heart thundering, Sara grabbed Maria's legs and forced her back from the bed. She grabbed for the syringe, knocking it away from her son.

*Please don't let any poison be injected.*

By now, Nico sat up on his knees, eyes wide, sobbing uncontrollably. Sara longed to offer comfort but she was locked in a struggle with the wild and furious nurse. Arms around the woman's waist, she tried to pull Maria as far away from Nico as possible.

"He must die," Maria groaned, pounding at Sara's hands, straining toward the little prince. "Your son must die."

Stunned that Maria knew of Nico's parentage, Sara's grip

went slack. The nurse whirled and slammed a fist into her still-tender side. A groan of pain *oomphed* from Sara. She doubled over.

With what little breath she had, she yelled, "Run, Nico! Run to Papa. Run!"

Though he had to be terrified, the little prince obeyed, his short legs flying over the floor. Maria lunged for him, screaming like a madwoman.

Though hurting and breathless, Sara grabbed for the woman's knees, pulling her down. They grappled on the floor. Maria quickly gained the upper hand. Somehow she'd retrieved the needle. She jabbed at Sara. Sara dodged to one side but not before the sting grazed her neck.

"Why did you come here? Why did you interfere? It would be over now." Maria slammed another vicious blow into Sara's side. Air whooshed from Sara in a scream of agony. Tears blinded her eyes. She struck out with her fingernails, clawing at Maria's face. Maria's strong fingers closed around her throat. Astraddle Sara's chest, she leaned in close, spittle appearing at the corners of her mouth. "Die in his place. The mighty prince will suffer either way. He will suffer as I have suffered."

The woman was raving mad. And insanely strong. She squeezed Sara's throat and with a gleam of sadistic pleasure in dark, Carvainian eyes watched her adversary struggle for breath.

Spots danced before Sara's eyes. She clawed at the larger woman's hands to no avail. Her head throbbed. She was dying.

But her son was safe. Aleks was safe. Even if she died, Maria's insane vendetta would end here and now.

A deeper darkness than she'd ever known began to close in. Maria's rambling tirade against Aleks went on and on, but Sara could no longer comprehend. Her hands went lax. A quiet humming filled her ears.

Suddenly, light flooded the room and the terrible pressure disappeared. Sara coughed and instinctively rolled to one side, knees drawn up.

Maria's stream of obscene ramblings increased, but she didn't touch Sara again.

Forcing her eyes open, Sara saw Aleks restraining the woman. Maria kicked and thrashed and spat. Face grim and full of sorrow, Aleks simply held her and let her rage.

"Murderer, murderer! You killed my son. You deserve to suffer the way I have. A son for a son. A son for a son."

The thunder of footsteps shook the floor as a host of security guards rushed in to take charge. Maria's cries of "a son for a son" echoed in the corridor as she was dragged away.

Certain now that Nico was safe, Sara let the blessed darkness overtake her.

# CHAPTER THIRTEEN

ADRENALINE JACKING from every pore, Aleks fell to his knees beside the red-haired woman. Curled in a fetal position, she was unconscious. Blood oozed from scrapes on her face and neck, and bruises in the shape of fingers already formed around her throat. But she lived. Thank God, she lived.

He shuddered to think what might have happened had he not been sleepless tonight. When he'd heard Nico's cry for help, he'd known something terrible was happening and had not hesitated.

"Sara." Heart in his throat, he scooped her easily into his arms, cradling her against his body as he would a child. "Sara, my love. Sara, my love."

His voice broke. She'd always been his love and out of fear and stupidity, he'd rejected the best thing, other than Nico, that had ever happened in his life. All this time she'd been correct about Maria. Was she correct about other things, as well?

Her eyelashes fluttered. Her mouth barely moved.

"Nico?" she said through a throat hoarse from trauma.

Aleks's insides ached. A nightmare had unfolded but he was wide-awake. Thank God Sara had not given up. "He is safe with his grandmother and a host of bodyguards. No one will get near him. You have my word."

"Check his blood. She stabbed him. The needle. I think I got it in time. Be sure."

Aleks cast a quick look around the floor and saw a filled syringe resting against the leg of the chair. The pounding in his head increased.

"Landish," he said to one of the remaining bodyguards. "Take that syringe to Dr. Konstantine. Tell him Nico may have been injected."

"Done." The man was gone in seconds.

Relief flickered through Sara's sea-blue eyes before she closed them again.

Around him, the remaining pair of bodyguards stood, normally placid faces furious at this affront on their ability to protect the castle. He understood. Sometimes a man failed to protect what mattered most.

"I will take Miss Presley to my apartment. When Dr. Konstantine is available, ask him to come to her. She needs attention."

If the men thought anything unusual about the royal prince taking a woman to his rooms, they didn't show it. One left straightaway while the other trailed Aleks down the corridor to stand guard outside the door. Aleks thought the effort useless at this point. The threat was over, but tonight was not the time to address the security breach. They had erred, but so had he.

Carrying Sara through to his sleeping area, he gently placed her on the bed. She was beautiful beyond words, inside and out. Why had he ever doubted her?

"Ah, my Sara, I am a fool."

Just then, Dr. Konstantine bustled in, hair sprouting in all directions. "By the heavens, Your Majesty, what is going on here tonight?"

"Did you receive the message about the syringe?"

"Still full. But I have ordered blood work to be certain. I cannot believe Maria is responsible. Tell me this is false."

"I wish I could."

Aleks apprised the physician of what he knew. He still could not fathom the kind and smiling mother of his best friend as a murderess. The truth wounded like a poison arrow.

"Security is questioning Maria but she seemed completely deranged." And he had been completely duped by her smiling pretense. Maria's grief had festered into hatred, poisoning her mind and heart. "I doubt they'll determine much tonight. For now, I must go to Nico and the queen and assure them that the threat is over." And to assure himself that his son had, indeed, escaped further harm.

"Go then, I'll take good care of your woman."

Aleks was halfway out the door before he realized what the doctor had said.

Sara awakened in a strange room. Her body ached all over, and she could barely swallow. She touched her throat. Was she coming down with the flu?

As she pushed back the fluffy covers, the events of last night flooded in. Her pulse bumped.

"Nico," she whispered.

She grabbed for the telephone beside the bed and dialed Aleks's private number. When he answered, she blurted through a raspy voice, "Is Nico all right?"

A pause on the other end. "You are awake?"

Obviously. "Nico? Tell me."

"He is well and full of an adventurous tale of a brave woman who saved him from the bad nurse." Aleks's tone was tired and sad. "He is in the next room having breakfast with his grandmother."

"Thank God."

"Indeed. You can be proud of your son. He sounded the alarm. But if not for you…" His voice trailed off. He cleared it.

Sara gripped the receiver, reliving last night's close call. "We were fortunate Maria decided to make her move before I left Carvainia."

"It was not luck. According to her confession, a rendering that made my blood run cold, she overheard our argument yesterday. She had planned to poison Nico over a period of months and force me to sit by helplessly as he died."

"Why did she change her mind?"

"You."

"Me?"

"She intended to administer the final overdose last night and leave evidence blaming you. You and I were already at odds. You were the obvious outsider. She had somehow learned of your relationship to Nico…and to me. She thought we would believe you had poisoned Nico as payback for revoking your visa."

"I would be blamed, and you would be punished."

He emitted a tired sigh. "Her revenge knew no bounds."

Sara's heart ached for him. "She truly is deranged."

"Yes." His voice was sad. "She even knew of a secret passage in the medical wing."

Sara gasped. "So I did see her go into Nico's room that time?"

"Yes. She laughed, rather maniacally I might add, because you'd seen her and no one believed you. I had no idea she hated me. None. And yet, you saw what I couldn't."

"I saw because I *am* an outsider, Aleks." A fact that pained her no end. "Your loyalty to Carlo's memory blinded you."

"Emotion. How does a leader separate emotion from reason?"

She had no answer for him. And in truth, one of the things she loved about him was his depth of feeling. No matter how hard he tried to hide it, he cared deeply. "What will happen to Maria?"

He drew in a long, quivering breath. "No matter what she's done, she is still the mother of the man who saved my life, a man who was my best friend. For him, I will take care of her."

"I expected no less."

If her sentiment surprised him, he didn't react. "There is an exceptional facility in Switzerland. She is on her way there, under heavy guard and sedation, of course. She will receive excellent care, but she will never be released."

"You must be shattered."

"I have suffered worse. Much worse." But he didn't elaborate. Instead he said, "I will send breakfast and Antonia to you. Rest. Last night was terrible for all of us, but for you most of all."

"But, I'm leaving today."

There was that pause again. "We need to talk. I will be up soon."

Before she could respond, he hung up.

An hour later, after she'd eaten and dressed, Sara paced the apartment, aware that Aleks had brought her to his room last night. But he had not slept here. Why had he done so? And what did he mean when he'd said they needed to talk?

Did she dare hope that he'd let her remain in Carvainia in some capacity? Perhaps as a nanny or a maid? At this point, she'd do anything to be near her son—and the man she loved.

Penny would call her a blind doormat, but she would rather be a servant here with the people she loved than alone in her Kansas bookshop.

A soft knock sounded on the outer door. She hurried to open it, finding both Aleks and his mother outside. She shrank back. Was this a two-pronged attack?

"May we come in?" Aleks asked, his expression giving nothing away.

Regardless of the grave situation, Sara couldn't help herself. "Considering this is your apartment, I suppose so."

She stepped aside and let them enter, trailing along, as tense as a bowstring as they went into the living quarters. The room was tastefully sumptuous, as befitted a prince, but the only thing in it that mattered to Sara was the prince himself.

The two women chose sofas opposite one another. Sara perched on the cushion edge, anxious and uncertain. The queen smoothed the unwrinkled hem of her suit skirt and sat with stiff, boarding school posture. As though purposefully choosing a neutral position, Aleks took a chair at one end between the two women.

The tension in the room was nearly visible.

Queen Irena spoke first. "I don't expect you to welcome me, Miss Presley. But you must hear the truth before you do anything else."

The queen, whose nose was normally raised in distaste, seemed subdued this morning. Her hands twisted in her lap, worrying an elegant, crested handkerchief. Black eyes, filled with loathing only yesterday, now swam with some other emotion.

Sara glanced from the queen to Aleks and back again. "The truth about what?"

"That's what we've come to talk with you about, Sara," Aleks said. "My mother and I had a long conversation this morning. She has something to tell you. And so do I."

In fisted hand, Irena's handkerchief went to her lips. A sob broke through, stunning Sara. The stiff-necked queen was crying? In the presence of a peasant?

"I have done you a great disservice," Irena said with a wobbly voice. She glanced at Aleks, eyes full of sorrow. "Both of you. Five years ago, Aleks was at war. He could not stop thinking and worrying about the red-haired American he had left behind. He could not come to you himself, so he sent me as his envoy."

Sara sucked in a stunned gasp. Her gaze flew to Aleks. "You were telling the truth?"

"Yes." His look was grim. "And there is more."

"You must understand, Miss Presley, I had nothing against you personally but you are not Carvainian. You are not of royal lineage. I could not allow my son, the ruler of a great nation, to marry a common American."

Sara's hand went to her throat. The ramifications of the queen's confession ricocheted through her. Aleks had not lied. He *had* loved her. He had tried to contact her.

She began to tremble with a great and terrible sorrow.

But the queen was not finished. "When I discovered the pregnancy, I went to great lengths to obtain the child. A beautiful son would be enough to soothe Aleksandre's pain when he learned of your rejection."

"But I didn't—I never—"

Queen Irena lifted an elegant hand. "No, you did not, but Prince Aleksandre believed you did. I told him this and many other untruths about you, including the payment you exacted for the sale of your child. You must believe me. I thought I was doing the right thing for everyone. For my country, my son and my grandson."

"And for yourself?"

Fresh tears sailed down Irena's proud face. "Can you forgive me?"

On shaky legs, Sara rose and moved away from the queen's pleading gaze. Forgive? How did she forgive such a wrong? How did she put aside the ocean of tears and the months of depression?

"I never fed him a bottle," she murmured, as much to herself as to the present company. "I wasn't there for his first steps. Or his first words."

She'd only dreamed about them, imagining each and every milestone.

"I am sorry, so very sorry."

"All that time Aleks hated me. He believed the worst lie of all. He thought I did not want him or his son." Glaring at the queen, Sara squeezed both hands against her bursting chest. "*Our* son."

With a soft groan, Aleks bolted from the chair and moved to the fireplace where he braced both hands against the stone mantel.

Queen Irena's dark gaze followed her son. "Prince Aleksandre has never hated you, my dear. That has been the problem. He wanted to hate you. I wanted him to. But he could not." She patted her cheeks with the handkerchief. "Please, come and sit. Hear me out. If you judge me harshly, it is no more than I deserve. But you must hear what I have to say—all of it."

Agitated, but relieved that the truth was finally coming to light, Sara did as Irena asked. Her stomach cramped and her back still hurt from fighting Maria, but an odd kind of hope kept sprouting up inside her like a persistent weed that simply would not give up and die.

"I failed my son and my grandson," Irena went on. "Both then and now. During the months since your arrival, I have been so focused on ridding the castle of your presence lest

Aleksandre discover my deception, that I did not see the danger to Nico. You saw it." Reaching out, she leaned forward as if to touch Sara's knee. "A mother knows things with her heart that others cannot see."

Sara knew the words were true. Her heart had known something was wrong, even when she'd had no solid evidence. "Yes. I knew. Somehow I knew."

"I am grateful beyond words, Sara Presley. If not for your persistence and determination and yes, your love, Nico may have died." She choked on a sob and took a moment to compose herself.

Tears welled in Sara's eyes, too. "Last night could have been worse. Maria could have succeeded."

"Except for your bravery, she would have." Haughtiness gone, the queen rose, still worrying the now-wrinkled and damp handkerchief. "That is why I am here this morning. I deeply regret my actions as well as my arrogant pride and elitism. I was wrong. A queen is not made by blood. She is made by strength of character and her love of country and of her prince. You will make a far better queen than I."

With a deep, sweeping curtsy that stunned Sara and left Aleks gaping, Queen Irena took her leave.

As the door whispered shut, Sara murmured, "What just happened?"

Aleks pushed away from the fireplace. "I have only seen her this broken once before—when my father died. My mother did us both a terrible disservice, Sara, but she is a fine woman and a good queen."

"She loves her princes very much." It was the only concession Sara was ready to give to a woman who had ruined her life.

"Indeed. She loves us enough to do anything to protect us, even if we do not wish to be protected."

In a way, Sara understood. Didn't she feel this way about Nico? "But all these years, you believed a lie about me."

"A fact I deeply regret. Though this is no excuse, the months after I returned from war were a terrible time. I was wounded and angry. I'd lost my dearest friend and thousands of fine warriors. My father was recently dead. My country was in postwar chaos and I was her young and inexperienced leader. Being betrayed by the only woman I'd ever loved seemed to fit into the general theme of my life. Without our son to live for, that would have been a hopeless time."

"No, Aleks. Even without Nico, you would have served your people well. You would have turned Carvainia into the thriving, beautiful place it is today. You are a born leader." A reminder of her commoner status. Aleks was born to the throne and required a woman of equal quality. She was born a nobody.

He smiled a little. "So, you like my country?"

"I love it." Just as I love you, she thought. But she didn't say as much. Instead she spoke of the one wish he might grant. "I want to stay in Carvainia."

"This is good to know because I have something to discuss with you."

"About?"

"Nico's future."

Sara's chin went up. "I want to be in that future, Aleks. Don't deny me that, not now when you know how much I love him."

"And what do I get in exchange?"

"Whatever it takes. Anything you ask."

"Anything?" His eyes twinkled. "Why, Sara, you have no idea what a man of my stature might require of such a beautiful, desirable woman."

She shook her head. "It doesn't matter. I'll do anything. I love my son that much."

"And what of the father?" His face became intense. "Do you still love the father as you once did? For you cannot deny that. I know now that you loved me."

Hopeful about the undercurrent flowing between them, Sara could answer with nothing less than the truth. "Yes. I do."

A soft sigh issued from his broad chest. He slid to one knee in front of her, clasping her hands in his. "Sara Presley, my beautiful, courageous, red-haired woman, mother of my child, heart of my heart, I, who was a blind man, will be blind no longer. I love you, too. No lies or raging anger could ever remove the wanting from my soul. I will want you until I die."

Heart lifting with each beautiful word, Sara touched her beloved's cheek. "But I'm not a Carvainian. I'm not royal."

"Those are my mother's requirements, not mine, and certainly not the rules of this nation. Carvainia needs *you* for her queen. Nico needs his mother. And the Prince of Carvainia requires a brave and fearless red-haired wife. Will you be that woman, Sara Presley? Will you grant me my fondest desire and marry me?"

Head reeling, heart thundering like a Kansas tornado, Sara opened her mouth to speak, but before she could say a word, the door slammed backward on its hinges.

Aleks bolted up to his feet, stance protective.

And then he laughed.

The most beautiful little boy in the world rushed inside the elegant room and threw his arms around Prince Aleksandre's legs. Earnest face turned upward, black eyes batting, he said, "Did you ask her, Papa? Did she say yes?"

Voice amused, Aleks stroked his son's hair. "I asked, but she has not given me an answer."

Nico's eyebrows furrowed in bewilderment. "But she must say yes, Papa. It was my fondest wish. I wished in the garden and I never, ever told."

By now, Sara vacillated between laughter and tears. She pressed her fingers against trembling lips.

"Yours, too?" Aleks asked with mock gravity. "Then, come, we must convince her together." The warrior prince returned to one knee and drew Nico down with him. "Now, you on the other side. A proposal must be done properly."

Adorably serious, Nico imitated his father, one knee on the floor and his tiny hand reaching for one of Sara's. The sweetness of the moment wrapped around her, warm and beautiful, a moment in time to capture for eternity. Her son. Her man. What more could she ask of life?

"We're waiting for an answer, Sara." Aleks's deep baritone was warm with love, the cold facade of Prince Aleksandre completely gone. "Will you marry us?"

Nico shot his father an exasperated look. "Wait, Papa. What about the Mama part?"

Sara's pulse stuttered. Did Nico know? Her gaze flew to Aleks. He nodded. "I told him that his mother—*you*—had been separated from us during the terrible war, but that you had finally found him again when he needed you most."

The tears shimmering on Sara's eyelashes broke loose. "I have looked for you for such a long, long time, Nico. For you and your Papa."

"Now that you're home, don't ever leave us again. Okay?"

This was the moment she'd dreamed of but never believed would happen, and all she could manage was, "Okay."

# EPILOGUE

*Six months later*

THE WEDDING OF THE CENTURY took place on a day when the sun was ordered to shine, the sea instructed to remain calm and blue, and every flower in Carvainia was expected to bloom.

Heart thundering in his chest, Aleks stood at the top of the left staircase, looking across the wide expanse of ancient, shining hall to his bride on the opposite side. After all that happened, he'd never expected to see this moment, but there she was. It was his first glimpse at her wedding dress, an American custom he found amusing. He'd seen everything else about her. Why not her wedding dress?

But Sara was worth the wait. Resplendent in creamy satin that nipped her narrow waist and hinted at her luscious curves, Sara was as regal as any royal-born queen. In a gesture that had touched him deeply, she had accepted his mother's offer to wear the simple diamond tiara Irena had worn in her own wedding. The concession gave him hope that the two could become friends.

Beneath the tiara, Sara's cinnamon-red hair was a crown of glory from which flowed gauzy layers of double veil as featherlight and airy as a Carvainian spring. She moved, flowing toward the steps, one hand on the banister, her glowing face turned toward him.

Aleks dipped his chin, unable to keep the smile from blooming. His wedding would not be a stiff and emotionless event, joining two royal houses. His was a wedding of love. He had every right to smile.

Sara smiled, too, and holding each other's gaze, they took the steps in unison. Sara's long train followed, a frothy, elegant entourage befitting his bride.

At the bottom, they turned together and met in the center hall. In this final moment of semiprivacy, with only the uniformed doormen waiting at the huge double doors, Aleks took the tips of her cold fingers and gently drew his bride to him.

"Shall I muss your lipstick?"

Her glossy-peach mouth curved. "Please do."

He did.

"What will the photographers think?" she asked, eyes shining with a love that was all his.

"They will know their prince married for love."

Carvainians had rejoiced at the announced engagement, though some expressed concern that Sara was not of royal lineage and brought nothing with her to the country. Aleks knew better. He'd left his heart in America. She'd brought it back.

"Your people await," she whispered, and he saw her nerves. They'd chosen a very public ceremony on a yacht in the harbor so that as many Carvainians who wished could attend the nuptials. Afterward, they would sail along the coastline for a day to greet thousands of others before heading out to sea for a much-anticipated honeymoon.

"*Our* people await," he corrected. Holding her soft, chilled hand in his, he started forward, eager to claim his bride.

\* \* \*

The massive doors swung wide and the noise rushed in. Sara vacillated between incredible joy and pure terror. She'd have preferred a quiet wedding in the children's garden or the family chapel, but she understood the important symbolism of this public ceremony on Aleks's beloved sea.

In the days since the announced engagement, she had become a public figure, meeting and greeting at dozens of functions around the beautiful little nation. The Carvainian people had welcomed her, accepting Aleks's choice, and she was determined to give them a loving and kind queen.

Besides, what woman didn't dream of a wedding so grand and perfect with a handsome prince at her side? Even cynical Penny had been won over by Aleks's charm.

Scanning the ship's deck, she searched for her friend and spotted the shining blond head, bouncing up and down like a rubber ball. Yes, Penny was here and as excited as a puppy. Aleks had brought everyone that mattered, though the American contingent was small, a handful of friends and a few distant cousins who had kept in contact after her mother had died.

There was nothing left in America to return to, even if she'd wanted to go back. Everything she loved was here.

Penny was now the sole owner of the bookstore, for a sum of one America dollar, though Sara would visit. After all, she'd promised Nico some wonderful books.

Sara squeezed Aleks's fingers and he winked at her. She laughed, partly from nerves but mostly from happiness.

Cheers and applause swelled as the wedding couple exited the castle and began walking the long path down to the sea. Military men and women in crisp white uniforms lined the pathway. The crowd, huge as it was, remained polite behind the low, decorative barriers, though flashbulbs snapped at a constant rate.

A red carpet sprinkled with a rainbow of tiny flowers led the way down to the shore and the moored yacht where the wedding party was already in place.

Sara's magnificent train trailed behind her for yards, held up by eight young ladies, four on each side. Half of the dark-haired girls were commoners, the other half of the royal line, but all had been selected for their good deeds and not for their last names. The announcement had pleased the Carvainian press, who heralded their soon-to-be queen as a friend to all. And that's exactly what she wanted to be.

From a flatboat in the harbor, a military band, their instruments glistening in the sunshine, played the Carvainian national anthem as Sara and Aleks proceeded across the lawn. All around the yacht, a flotilla of flower-bedecked boats bobbed gently on the serene sea.

With sabers drawn and resting at their sides, military attendants, stiff and proper in white uniforms, lined the boardwalk up onto the ship. This was Aleks's honor guard, a group of men with whom he'd served. As the couple passed, the men snapped the sabers to their shoulders, symbolically ready to defend and protect their prince and his bride. Sara felt Aleks's quiver and understood his emotion. He loved these men, as they loved him.

In the months of the betrothal she'd learned much about the man she was about to marry. He was a loving father, a good son, a true and worthy prince who grieved for the loss of his soldiers and provided generously for their families. He ruled his nation with a gentle hand and a wise heart.

She was proud and blessed to join herself to such a man.

As they ascended to the deck and the waiting wedding

party, Aleks held her elbow. She was glad for the support because her knees wobbled. In this surreal moment, the swell of music and people and the smell of ocean and flowers overwhelmed her senses.

"Papa, Mama." Nico's whisper came to her through all the noise. She turned to find his wide, white smile and excited black eyes peering at her from beside Queen Irena.

Irena guided the little prince forward. He was dressed in white tails and crimson cravat exactly like his father's. Together the pair was stunning. Her love for them left her breathless.

She held out a hand, embarrassed to see it tremble. Nico wiggled into place between her and Aleks. The three of them stood beneath an arch of feather flags, white-columned banners of sheer fabric billowing in the sea breeze. The clergyman, decked in long, flowing robes of crimson and cream, began the ceremony.

Even with thousands of spectators crowding the shoreline and spreading up over the hillsides, a reverent hush fell, broken only by the lap of water and an occasional birdcall.

Beautiful, though unfamiliar words were spoken joining Prince Aleksandre Lucian Domenico d'Gabriel with Sara Elizabeth Presley. And though the pomp and ceremony went on for a while, Sara lost track of time as she treasured every word, every Carvainian tradition kept, every glimpse into her beloved's eyes.

And then it was over and Aleks reached for her.

"This is an American tradition I must keep," he said, a half grin on his face as he kissed her.

A shout of approval went up from the shore but was drowned out by a deafening roar overhead. Bemused and happy, Sara held tight to Aleks's hand as they raised their faces to the sky. A precision team of Carvainian Air Force jets swooped past, leaving a wake of red-and-white contrails to honor their prince and his bride. As the planes disappeared from sight, fireworks exploded in a kaleidoscope of color against a backdrop of blue sky and fair sea.

"In my loneliest hours," Aleks said, gazing down at her with a look that melted her bones, "I pictured you here exactly like this."

She laughed softly. "In my wildest dreams I never imagined *anything* like this. You a prince. The two of us married. Here with our son."

"Would you have dreamed it if you'd known?"

"Oh, yes." She cupped his firm, smooth jaw. "My dreams were always of you, no matter who you are or where you live. The man you are inside is the man I love."

Heedless of the crowd, he drew her close again. She placed a hand against his strong, warrior's heart, content to know that it beat for her.

Cameras flashed. But they'd carved out these seconds of privacy and they would have them.

"Your love is a powerful thing, my queen. It has healed me. It has healed our son." He reached inside his jacket and withdrew an envelope. "I have a gift for you."

Curious, with shaky fingers, Sara opened the flap. Inside were the shredded bits of a million-dollar bank draft.

"I don't understand."

"I discovered it in my desk that night before Maria's attack on you and Nico."

"Before the attack? Then you knew—?"

"Yes, I knew you were sincere, that you had not agreed to the transplant for money. I was bewildered and broken and unable to sleep. That's why I was awake when Nico called for help. When I saw these scraps of paper, I knew I could never send you away. Even if my mother had told the truth, I couldn't let you go. Even if I was the worst kind of fool, I could not lose you again. You owned my heart. A warrior dies without his heart."

Tears prickled the back of her eyelids. "Oh Aleks. Of all the gifts you've given me, this one is the most beautiful."

With a smile, he bumped his forehead against hers. "That was exactly what I expected you to say." He arched his eyebrows toward the water. "Shall we?"

She caught his meaning instantly. "Yes, let's do."

Together they went to the railing, trailed by attendants and photographers. Each took a portion of the shredded paper, then joined hands, lifting them high. Nico ran to join them, raising both hands to clasp his parents' sleeves.

"No looking back," Sara said.

"Only to the future," Aleks added. "*Our* future."

And with a whoop of delight they released the offending bits of paper, letting the wind and sea carry them far, far away—along with the pain and sorrow and grief that had kept them apart for so long.

Across the way, the band struck up a rousing song of victory and exuberant joy.

The trio on the yacht, the prince, his queen and the little prince, fell into a satin and tulle embrace, laughing and crying all at once.

The past was over. Let the future begin.

\* \* \* \* \*

*Rancher Ramsey Westmoreland's temporary cook
is way too attractive for his liking.
Little does he know Chloe Burton came to his ranch
with another agenda entirely....*

That man across the street had to be, without a doubt, the most handsome man she'd ever seen.

Chloe Burton's pulse beat rhythmically as he stopped to talk to another man in front of a feed store. He was tall, dark and every inch of sexy—from his Stetson to the well-worn leather boots on his feet. And from the way his jeans and Western shirt fit his broad muscular shoulders, it was quite obvious he had everything it took to separate the men from the boys. The combination was enough to corrupt any woman's mind and had her weakening even from a distance. Her body felt flushed. It was hot. Unsettled.

Over the past year the only male who had gotten her time and attention had been the e-mail. That was simply pathetic, especially since now she was practically drooling simply at the sight of a man. Even his stance—both hands in his jeans pockets, legs braced apart, was a pose she would carry to her dreams.

And he was smiling, evidently enjoying the conversation being exchanged. He had dimples, incredibly sexy dimples in not one but both cheeks.

"What are you staring at, Clo?"

Chloe nearly jumped. She'd forgotten she had a lunch date. She glanced over the table at her best friend from college, Lucia Conyers.

"Take a look at that man across the street in the blue shirt, Lucia. Will he not be perfect for Denver's first issue of *Simply*

*Irresistible* or what?" Chloe asked with so much excitement she almost couldn't stand it.

She was the owner of *Simply Irresistible*, a magazine for today's up-and-coming woman. Their once-a-year Irresistible Man cover, which highlighted a man the magazine felt deserved the honor, had increased sales enough for Chloe to open a Denver office.

When Lucia didn't say anything but kept staring, Chloe's smile widened. "Well?"

Lucia glanced across the booth at her. "Since you asked, I'll tell you what I see. One of the Westmorelands—Ramsey Westmoreland. And yes, he'd be perfect for the cover, but he won't do it."

Chloe raised a brow. "He'd get paid for his services, of course."

Lucia laughed and shook her head. "Getting paid won't be the issue, Clo—Ramsey is one of the wealthiest sheep ranchers in this part of Colorado. But everyone knows what a private person he is. Trust me—he won't do it."

Chloe couldn't help but smile. The man was the epitome of what she was looking for in a magazine cover and she was determined that whatever it took, he would be it.

"Umm, I don't like that look on your face, Chloe. I've seen it before and know exactly what it means."

She watched as Ramsey Westmoreland entered the store with a swagger that made her almost breathless. She *would* be seeing him again.

*Look for Silhouette Desire's*
HOT WESTMORELAND NIGHTS *by Brenda Jackson,*
*available March 9 wherever books are sold.*

*Silhouette* *Desire*

## THE WESTMORELANDS

*NEW YORK TIMES*
bestselling author

# BRENDA JACKSON

## HOT WESTMORELAND NIGHTS

Ramsey Westmoreland knew better than to lust after the hired help. But Chloe, the new cook, was just so delectable. Though their affair was growing steamier, Chloe's motives became suspicious. And when he learned Chloe was carrying his child this Westmoreland Rancher had to choose between pride or duty.

*Available March 2010 wherever books are sold.*

**Always Powerful, Passionate and Provocative.**

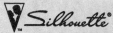

# LARGER-PRINT BOOKS!

## GET 2 FREE LARGER-PRINT NOVELS PLUS
## 2 FREE GIFTS!

### HARLEQUIN® *Romance.*

## From the Heart, For the Heart

---

**YES!** Please send me 2 FREE LARGER-PRINT Harlequin® Romance novels and my 2 FREE gifts (gifts are worth about $10). After receiving them, if I don't wish to receive any more books, I can return the shipping statement marked "cancel." If I don't cancel, I will receive 6 brand-new novels every month and be billed just $4.34 per book in the U.S. or $4.99 per book in Canada. That's a saving of almost 17% off the cover price! It's quite a bargain! Shipping and handling is just 50¢ per book in the U.S. and 75¢ per book in Canada.* I understand that accepting the 2 free books and gifts places me under no obligation to buy anything. I can always return a shipment and cancel at any time. Even if I never buy another book from Harlequin, the two free books and gifts are mine to keep forever.                     186 HDN E4HN    386 HDN E4HY

Name _____ (PLEASE PRINT) _____

Address _____ Apt. # _____

City _____ State/Prov. _____ Zip/Postal Code _____

Signature (if under 18, a parent or guardian must sign) _____

### Mail to the **Harlequin Reader Service:**
**IN U.S.A.:** P.O. Box 1867, Buffalo, NY  14240-1867
**IN CANADA:** P.O. Box 609, Fort Erie, Ontario  L2A 5X3

Not valid for current subscribers to Harlequin Romance Larger-Print books.

**Are you a current subscriber to Harlequin Romance books and want to receive the larger-print edition? Call 1-800-873-8635 today!**

\* Terms and prices subject to change without notice. Prices do not include applicable taxes. N.Y. residents add applicable sales tax. Canadian residents will be charged applicable provincial taxes and GST. Offer not valid in Quebec. This offer is limited to one order per household. All orders subject to approval. Credit or debit balances in a customer's account(s) may be offset by any other outstanding balance owed by or to the customer. Please allow 4 to 6 weeks for delivery. Offer available while quantities last.

**Your Privacy:** Harlequin Books is committed to protecting your privacy. Our Privacy Policy is available online at www.eHarlequin.com or upon request from the Reader Service. From time to time we make our lists of customers available to reputable third parties who may have a product or service of interest to you. If you would prefer we not share your name and address, please check here. ☐

**Help us get it right**—We strive for accurate, respectful and relevant communications. To clarify or modify your communication preferences, visit us at www.ReaderService.com/consumerschoice.

---

HRLP10

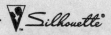

# SPECIAL EDITION

### FROM *USA TODAY* BESTSELLING AUTHOR
# CHRISTINE RIMMER

## A BRIDE FOR JERICHO BRAVO

Marnie Jones had long ago buried her wild-child impulses and opted to be "safe," romantically speaking. But one look at born rebel Jericho Bravo and she began to wonder if her thrill-seeking side was about to be revived. Because if ever there was a man worth taking a chance on, there he was, right within her grasp....

*Available in March
wherever books are sold.*